The Secret Dog

Born in Chicago, Joe Friedman has lived in London for many years, where he divides his time between writing and practising psychotherapy. He is author of the children's series Boobela and Worm, and in his spare time loves to do improvisation and story-telling.

THE SECRET DOG

JOE FRIEDMAN

Illustrated by
Tim Archbold

First published in 2015 by
Birlinn Limited
West Newington House
10 Newington Road
Edinburgh
EH9 1QS

www.birlinn.co.uk

ISBN: 978 1 78027 287 0

British Library Cataloguing-in-Publication Data
A catalogue record for this book is available from the British Library

Typeset by Iolaire Typesetting, Newtonmore
Printed and bound by Grafica Veneta
www.graficaveneta.com

For Joe and Yvonne

who provided me with the perfect
introduction to the Isle of Skye

Chapter 1

The sea eagle circled lazily far overhead. Its three-metre wingspan made it easily visible. Josh kept an eye on it, as his long legs carried him swiftly up the rough dirt path. He knew the predator's eyes were sharper than his.

As usual, he'd headed straight for the commons after school. He had several hours to himself. Time to explore, and to try to find animals who were injured or ill. Josh loved to nurse them back to health. His uncle didn't mind him bringing them home – as long as it was temporary. But he had an iron rule – no pets.

Suddenly, the eagle changed direction. Had it spotted an animal in trouble? Josh watched as the bird started to circle over an area to his left. He knew this didn't *necessarily* mean it had seen potential prey – but the hairs on the back of his neck prickled.

The bird seemed to be concentrating its attention on a steep grass-covered gully that led down to one of the many rivers that crossed the commons. The gully was pitted with muddy holes and odd-shaped gashes where erosion had eaten away the land. Because the commons didn't belong to anybody, nobody took much care of it.

Two thousand sheep called it home. Two thousand sheep, lots of small wild animals, and Josh.

Josh had been exploring the commons for five years, since he'd come to live on the island. He loved it all, every neglected bit of it.

The sea eagle had adjusted its flight path again. It was flying lower, and circling an area near the river below. If there *was* an animal to save, Josh hoped it wasn't on the other side. He hadn't changed out of his school uniform.

To his left there was a wire fence. He put his hand on a solid-looking fence-post and used it to vault over. Then he started down the steep slope, keeping an eye on the huge bird. It was circling still lower. Maybe it sensed Josh was a threat to its dinner.

As Josh got closer to the river, he looked from side to side, his eyes rapidly scanning the area for any signs of life. His long, dirty-blond hair flopped over his eyes. He hadn't noticed any breaks in the fence ... And surely he'd *see* a sheep in trouble. The sea eagle must be homing in on something smaller.

The river level wasn't at its highest point – the winter snow from the top of the hills had already melted and passed through, but it was still flowing pretty rapidly. He hastened along the bank. The eagle was still circling. *What was it looking at?*

Then Josh saw a slight movement, under a bush on the other side of the river where the bank was lowest. He couldn't see what was making the bush move. But if it was just the wind, a sea eagle wouldn't be so interested.

He glanced at his school shoes and trousers. *Why did it have to be on the other side?* But then, out of

the corner of his eye, he saw the sea eagle climb. Josh knew what that meant. It was getting ready to strike.

Without thinking, Josh charged into the river. The icy water made him catch his breath. It filled his shoes and soaked his trousers but he didn't hesitate. He knew he only had seconds to save the sea eagle's prey. His right foot slipped on one of the slick stones at the bottom of the river and he started to lose his balance. But he managed to plant his left on some gravel and kept going.

The sea eagle started to dive. Josh was out of time. He lunged forward. He tripped on the low bank but his momentum carried him into the bush. Thorns tore at his face. He was dimly aware of the sea eagle veering off, making a series of short, frustrated yaps. And then he saw what the bird was after.

It was a little bundle of soaking fur. A hedgehog? No. His eyes widened. It was a puppy! A black and white Border collie, shivering with cold.

'Did you fall in the river?' Josh wondered aloud. Then he understood: puppies this small didn't stray far from their mothers, who didn't go near rivers. He hadn't fallen. Someone must have thrown the dog into the river to get rid of it.

'I bet you were the runt of the litter,' he spoke softly, knowing his voice would calm the dog. He imagined the puppy pulling himself onto the bank with a huge effort for something so tiny. Josh's heart went out to him. 'You're a brave little soul,' he said.

Gently, he put his hand underneath the dog. He gasped.

'You're like a bag of frozen peas! You must have been in the water for ages! I'll have to get you warm. Right away.' Then Josh realised the puppy wasn't a "he". It was a "she"!

Carefully, he crawled backwards out of the bush, trying to limit the damage to his face and clothing. Holding the puppy in both hands, he crossed the river. Once he was safely on the other side, he cradled her in one hand, lifted his sweater and started to undo the middle buttons of his shirt.

She nuzzled up against his chest. Her nose was icy! He'd saved many animals, but never one that was this far gone. Surely he couldn't have found her too late!

His mind raced. If she was going to survive, he had to get her dry and then some warm food in her tummy. He glanced at his watch. His uncle, Calum, wouldn't be home yet, surely. He'd be out doing something on their small farm.

That would give him a chance to hide the puppy, and to get his trousers in the washing machine and his shoes in the airing cupboard.

Still holding the sodden collie against his skin, Josh buttoned up his shirt as far as he could. He turned and, squelching with every step, raced towards home.

Chapter 2

Josh put the pup on the dark kitchen counter as he stripped off his trousers and threw them in the dryer. He'd already put his shoes in the airing cupboard. He wasn't optimistic they'd be dry by the time he had to leave for school the next morning.

He put a pan of milk on the Aga to heat, then rushed to the bathroom where he found a towel and tied it around his waist. Then, back to the stove, where the milk was just starting to boil around the edges. He poured it into a mug. Holding it in one hand and the puppy in the other, he headed for the ladder to his room in the loft. At the bottom of the ladder, he hesitated. He'd have to climb without hands . . .

Okay. He'd use the hand holding the mug to balance. As his head went through the opening into his room, a waft of warm air hit him. The loft baked in high summer and froze in the winter. In June, it could go either way. Normally, when it was this hot, the first thing he'd do was open the velux window. But today, hot was good. Hot was exactly what the vet ordered.

He laid the pup down on his blanket, and put the milk on the wooden crate that served as his bedside table. He untied the towel and started to touch-dry

the puppy's fur. Then he picked up the mug and put it up to the pup's black nose. She turned away and looked at him out of the corner of her eye. 'What's this about?' she seemed to be asking.

'Let me show you,' Josh said, a smile in his voice. He stuck his finger in the warm milk, and held it up to her mouth. After a moment, a tiny tongue came out and licked it. It felt lovely and rough against his skin. The puppy glanced at him again. Then her tongue started going in and out of the milk.

Josh didn't let her have too much. He'd learned the hard way that small animals never know when to stop eating – he'd once let a starving rabbit eat too much and it had been violently sick all over his school uniform. As soon as he removed the mug, the puppy curled up into a ball the size of a small grape-fruit. In a moment she was fast asleep, exhausted by her ordeal. Tenderly, Josh wrapped her in his wool blanket.

He sat beside her, with his hand gently resting on her sleeping form. He had to think. Calum would be home in a few minutes. He needed a plan.

But here Josh ran into a brick wall. He already knew his uncle's position on pets. They were for people with more money than sense. Crofters like them could only afford to keep working animals.

Josh felt the puppy stir under his hand. Maybe she was having a dream? He imagined her struggling to keep her head above the freezing water, desperately searching for a place where the bank was low, seizing her chance and scrambling up onto it . . . And then he came by, just as the sea eagle spotted her. It was fate. He was *meant* to have her!

If she lived . . . She had to live!

From his experience with other animals he'd rescued, Josh knew the next couple of days were critical. The puppy's heart might have been too stressed by the freezing water, or her body might have used up too much energy fighting the cold. An infection might get hold of her weakened immune system . . . But with his help, surely none of those things would happen. She'd recover fully.

He heard the back door close downstairs. He had to go to help with dinner. And to convince Calum to let him keep her.

Josh sat across from his uncle, at the small dark wooden table that served as their dining room. Dinner was a mutton stew, which had been cooking on the Aga all day. Mutton stew could be kept going for days with the addition of carrots, potatoes and whatever other vegetables came into season from their garden. It wasn't usual summer fare, but summer didn't guarantee warmth this far north. And Josh was used to it.

It was still light outside but the kitchen didn't have very big windows. The old cabinets, new when his uncle was a child, didn't lend much cheer. They ate in a kind of low-level gloom. The maroon Aga in the corner was the only thing that added some colour. It was one of Josh's jobs to keep it fed with wood, and to bank it down at night.

They ate in silence, as usual. Calum was a

middle-aged man, bald on top with dark brown hair around the sides. Very fit, like most crofters, he was roughly the same height as Josh, but thicker around the chest and waist. He was a man of few words. There were some topics he got animated about: the animals on the farm, subsidies for cattle and Josh's school reports. But none of these seemed to be on his mind that evening. He hadn't even noticed the cuts on Josh's face.

Usually Josh didn't mind the quiet. But today he had to bring something up. And the silence made it more difficult for him to make it seem casual. His mind dashed in one direction and then another. What could he say to persuade his uncle to let him keep the puppy?

Calum had almost finished his stew. In a moment, he'd push his chair away from the table and go into the living room to read the local paper. It was now or never.

'If someone gave me a dog,' Josh started. Then he realised his uncle, who was slightly deaf, hadn't heard him. He started again, speaking louder. 'If someone gave me a dog, could I keep it?'

Was that it? That was the best he could do? *If someone gave me a dog could I keep it?* Josh was furious with himself. 'I mean we could call it a birthday present. A birthday present and a Christmas present,' he added quickly.

It was a while before his uncle responded. Josh desperately cast around for something to make his request more compelling. Nothing came to him.

'Animals cost money,' Calum spoke softly. 'And we're already struggling. Maybe when we have a good year.'

That was no help! The list of things that would arrive when they had 'a good year' was already long. It included a skateboard, a mobile phone, a computer and a bigger window for the loft.

'I'll earn the money to feed it!' Josh pleaded.

'Your priority is improving your school grades,' Calum said firmly. 'And there's little enough work around here for grown-ups, let alone twelve-year-old boys.'

'You just don't think I'd take good care of it,' Josh said, sullenly.

His uncle frowned. 'Don't ever think that, lad. I've seen how you are with the animals on the farm. And the wee ones you bring home. It's just that it's hard enough for me to provide you with the necessaries. A pet would be a luxury for us.'

Josh was sure that if he'd been cleverer, he could have come up with an argument that would have persuaded his uncle. But now it was too late. Once his uncle had decided something, he'd stubbornly refuse to change his mind.

'All right,' Josh said. He stood to clear the table.

'All right' just meant that he wasn't going to argue further. Not that he wasn't going to keep the puppy. He was determined to do that, whatever it took.

Chapter 3

Josh had been looking forward to seeing the puppy all day. By the time school finished, he'd decided he couldn't wait another moment. Running the two miles home wasn't a problem. But it did mean he'd have to pass Yvonne and Kearney, two classmates who followed the same path as him, at least most of the way home. He was a bit scared of them, but for different reasons. He was frightened of Yvonne, a brown-haired, intense girl, because she was so smart, and of Kearney because he was big and mean and the school bully.

'If it isn't our "blow-in"! What's the hurry, city boy?' Kearney shouted as he approached them. 'Catching a bus back to town?'

As usual, Josh was stuck for something to say in reply. Why hadn't he thought of anything in advance? He'd known he'd run into them. He searched his mind. Nothing. He just wasn't sharp like that. As he stepped off the path to pass them, he consoled himself. Perhaps it was for the best. If he said some-thing silly, Kearney would repeat it to everyone in the class. And if he said something clever, Kearney would probably hit him.

The encounter dented his good spirits, though, reminding him that, even after five years on the

island, people regarded him as a 'blow-in'. And that *he* didn't have anyone to walk home with . . .

Uncle Calum's small bungalow was halfway up a hill, about twenty metres south of the main road. Most of the houses around here were north of the road, higher up on the hill. They might be able to see further, but the view from his uncle's house was still pretty special. Below the house were a couple of fields, dotted with his uncle's Highland cattle and sheep. Beyond them was the old river bed, lined with trees. And beyond that, the beach to the loch, a large, dark body of water that ran all the way out to the Atlantic. Sometimes, they could see dolphins from their front window. Josh loved spotting them playing together.

*   *   *

Josh warmed a pan of milk. His puppy would be hungry. But as soon as he got to the top of the ladder, Josh knew something was wrong. He could hear the puppy's breathing. It was fast and irregular. He raced over to her. She was stretched out awkwardly on his pillow. Her nose was hot to the touch and her temperature was way too high. He couldn't wake her to take any of the warm milk he'd brought.

From his experience with other rescued animals, he knew she'd caught an infection. And that her small, weakened body would find it difficult to fight it. It was as if a heavy stone had rolled on top of his heart. His knees felt like buckling.

He fought to stay upright. 'I've been here before.'

He said it aloud, as if to remind himself that he would survive. But then hot anger surged through him. Why didn't anything go right for him? But there was no time to think about that now.

He had to act. He almost slid down the ladder in his haste to get to the kitchen. He returned immediately with a bag of frozen chips, tenderly lifted the unconscious puppy, and settled her onto his lap. Then he sat there, as the afternoon lengthened, cooling her down every few minutes with the slowly defrosting chips. But mostly, he talked to her.

He told her how he'd saved loads of animals, but that she was special. He was going to keep her forever.

'I've come up with a plan,' Josh told her softly. 'I'm going to train you to work with sheep! Once you're a *working* dog, everything will be different. Calum will accept you. And we'll roam the commons having adventures and searching for other animals to rescue. That's why you've *got* to get better!'

Then Josh started to tell her about himself. How when he was a toddler, his mother had always pointed to a photograph of a handsome soldier when he'd asked about his father . . . and that it was only when he was four that he'd come to understand that his dad had been killed in a far-away war before he'd been born. And that he would never meet or know him. All he had were his mother's stories about him and an album of pictures of his parents' wedding and honeymoon.

He checked the puppy's temperature. Still way too hot. He tucked the bag of frozen chips in next to her.

Then he told the puppy about his mother. How they had lived together in a tiny flat and how she was small and funny and warm and how she'd raised him all by herself and how they were just fine, the two of them ... until she'd decided to be a good Samaritan and drive a neighbour who was having a baby to the hospital. She must have been going way too fast – they were both killed instantly.

He was just seven at the time, and though he still had some photos of her, he just didn't seem to be able to remember her properly. Not *feel* inside him what she was like. Not since he'd come to the island ...

That had happened two days after the crash. His mother's brother, who he'd only met once when he was so small he couldn't remember it, had taken him in. But Calum wasn't at all like his mother. Not warm, not funny. He wasn't cruel or anything like that, he assured the sleeping puppy. It was just that he wasn't ... her.

Still – Josh remembered to check the puppy's temperature and remove the bag of chips – the one good thing about living here was that he'd discovered the commons, the wild and varied land near his uncle's croft. And it was there he'd discovered his passion: saving animals, like her.

It wasn't until the early evening that the puppy opened one of her eyes and with a huge effort, turned her little head to look up at him. She just gazed at

16

him and Josh felt a huge joy well up inside him. He *knew* then that she'd pull through.

And a name for her popped into his head – almost as if *she'd* put it there. Reggae. The music his mum had loved.

Chapter 4

It was the first class after lunch and the air in the Portakabin classroom was stale. Josh's desk was near the window, in the sun, and his head was muzzy. Reggae was still waking him in the night, even though she'd fully recovered from her infection.

She wasn't noisy, but she loved to climb all over his face. Just when he'd finally fallen deeply asleep. Josh guessed she needed attention. She was alone way too much, even though he usually ran home at lunch time and spent as much time as he could with her before and after school.

She was growing fast. Too fast. Josh knew he couldn't keep her secret in his room much longer. His uncle's hearing might not be the best, but his sense of smell was fine. And Reggae's pee plus the hot sun in the loft were a potent combination.

Mr Eldon, his geography teacher, was droning on. He insisted on talking about places on the other side of the world – when Josh wanted to understand the geography of the island where they lived. He knew it was fifty miles long, and that the loch his uncle lived on was roughly in the middle. But he didn't get how it had come to have so many different types of landscape in such a small area. It had mountains in one place and moors and lochs and cliffs in others.

Once, when he'd been bored – or brave – enough to ask about this, Mr Eldon had made fun of him, saying that Josh might have very limited horizons, but that other students were interested in the wider world. Looking at the blank faces around him, Josh didn't think this was true.

Josh stared out at the empty school grounds. A distinctive van was making its way along the road towards the village. It was the vet. His mind drifted back in time to the day, not long after he'd arrived on the island, when he'd first met him.

He had been wandering through the fields one afternoon when he'd heard a worrying sound. On the other side of a hillock he'd found Morag, one of his uncle's Highland cattle, lying on the ground, groaning in pain. She'd looked terrible. Her calf was lowing plaintively not far away. Josh had run to his uncle.

'Uncle Calum! Uncle Calum! Morag's not well!'

Josh led his uncle to the sick cow. Calum took one look and ran back home to phone the vet.

Josh knew even then that this meant it was serious. One of his uncle's favourite topics at the dinner table was how much the vet cost.

But there were only twenty cattle on the croft and losing one would be a major blow, especially Morag, who reliably produced a healthy calf every year.

The vet's distinctive van had arrived ten minutes later. The sides were brightly painted with scenes from the American old west: canyons, covered wagons, horses, Indians and an Indian village. A gruff-looking man with a trimmed white beard emerged wearing a cowboy hat. He greeted Calum with a warm hand-shake and then turned to Josh.

'Calum's nephew! I've heard a lot about you.'

Josh had just stared, quite unable to speak. The vet seemed like a larger-than-life hero out of a movie.

After waiting a moment for a response, the vet had simply tipped his hat to Josh, and then followed Calum to the field where Morag was still lying on the ground. Josh had trailed along behind the two men, not close enough to get in anybody's way and get told off, but not far enough to miss anything.

To Josh's surprise, the vet stopped some distance from Morag, who was twitching on the ground. He took in the situation.

'I think you're right. It's the staggers,' he'd said to Calum.

Then he'd turned and walked away as if he there were nothing urgent about the situation. But once the vet was about fifty metres from Morag, he ran back to the van. Josh followed and watched as the vet opened the rear door and climbed in. Josh's eyes opened wide. The back of the van was like a minia-ture operating theatre! There were shelves along the walls containing neat rows of medicines and a table covered with white paper. Along its side was an oxygen tank, and shiny medical-looking tools. The vet quickly picked up two small boxes, and two syringes – one big, one small – from a large box. Then he'd run back towards Morag. Josh had had to go at top speed to keep up.

But when he came within sight of the cow, the vet slowed to a walk. Why, Josh had wondered, didn't he run all the way to the cow? She was obviously in pain.

The vet stopped about ten metres away from Morag. He filled up the small syringe with medicine from one of the boxes. Then he crept up to the cow, knelt, stuck the needle into a vein in her neck, and swiftly retreated.

The vet must have noticed Josh was watching him. He said in a soft voice, 'That was a sedative, to calm her down. Her nervous system is in a terrible state, because she's depleted of magnesium. Any sudden movement could kill her.'

So that's why the vet walked slowly while he was close to Morag! He didn't want to alarm her. Josh liked that the vet had taken the trouble to explain, even though he didn't understand everything he'd said. The vet was filling up the second, much bigger, syringe. Josh could see that Morag wasn't twitching as much as before.

The vet walked slowly towards her, knelt and inserted the second needle into her vein. As soon as the syringe was empty, the vet retreated once again.

For a couple of minutes, nothing seemed to happen.

Calum was tense. 'Were we too late?' he asked in a low voice.

Then all of a sudden, Morag had almost jumped to her feet. Giving the three of them no more than a quick backward glance, she'd galloped off to join her calf.

To Josh, this had seemed little short of a miracle. It was as if the vet could raise the dead! *He* wanted to be able to do this too.

Suddenly Josh remembered where he was. Not in a field healing Highland cows, but a classroom. He looked around anxiously. Had anyone noticed him daydreaming?

It seemed not. He wished school were easier. Reception had been fine. But once teachers started writing on blackboards, he'd struggled to make sense of their sentences. For a while, he told himself it was their bad handwriting.

But this past year, new computer whiteboards had arrived. He still couldn't make out half the words, even when they were typed. Maybe it wasn't as many as half. But it was enough so that he couldn't figure out what sentences meant.

So geography wasn't horrible *just* because Mr Eldon was mean and boring. He also used the whiteboard a lot. Like his English, religious studies, history and citizenship teachers.

It wasn't that Josh didn't have plans to deal with this. He might not be able to read well but he wasn't an idiot. But his major tactic was still praying the teacher wouldn't call on him.

'Josh? Are you with us today?'

He'd drifted off again. Worrying what he was going to do about Reggae peeing in his bedroom.

'I'm sorry.' Apologising automatically was one of the things Josh did to try to make things better when he got called on.

'That's very nice, Josh,' Mr Eldon said sarcastically. 'But I'd prefer an answer to my question.'

Josh's eyes searched the classroom. There were a lot of faces looking in his direction. He noticed Kearney, who was smiling maliciously at him. He wished he had a friend. Someone's kind eyes would make these horrible moments easier.

'I think I must have missed the question.'

'That was the way it seemed to me too,' Mr Eldon said.

'Could you repeat it please?' Josh asked.

'I think not. Instead I'll give you a detention – a double detention – in the hope that next time you'll have some incentive to stay with us for the whole period.'

A double detention – that might mean his uncle would get home before Josh! Before he had a chance to clear away the newspapers soaked with dog pee . . . His uncle might find Reggae!

* * *

Josh ran all the way home, praying that his uncle hadn't come home early. He'd changed the newspapers in his room at lunch, but Reggae had drunk a lot of milk . . .

After taking off his shoes at the door, Josh rushed through the house. Then he breathed a sigh of relief. He was home first.

He climbed the ladder to his room, and then, holding his nose with one hand, he crumpled up the sodden newspaper with the other. Fortunately, he'd left the window open at lunchtime.

'I know it's horrible for you to be left alone. And with this stink,' he told her. 'At least you've managed to hit the paper. Most of the time.' He finished gathering the soggy paper up. Reggae looked at him eagerly. As far as she was concerned, now that he was home, it was time to play!

'Let me get rid of this first.'

Even with the loft window wide open, there was no mistaking the smell from the bottom of the ladder.

Why did dogs have to grow so quickly? She'd only been living with him a little over a month!

As he climbed back into the loft through the hatch in the floor, Reggae attempted to jump up on him. Her little legs were not quite up to the task. Josh had to catch her to keep her from falling.

'Careful!' he said. 'It's a long way down.'

Reggae gave him a cheeky look, as if to say 'I knew you'd catch me!'

'You think you're pretty smart,' Josh said with a smile in his voice.

Then he heard the front door close. That had been close.

'Josh, are you home?' his uncle called.

'Just got here,' Josh shouted down the hatch. He could hear his uncle walking past the ladder on the way to his room. Then he heard him stop.

'There's quite a pong coming from up there,' he said, and started to climb the ladder.

Josh felt the blood drain from his legs. He shoved

Reggae under the bedclothes and then rushed to meet his uncle, so he didn't come into the room. At least he'd cleared away the newspapers!

Calum stuck his head through the hatch.

'I know,' Josh said swiftly. 'I should have washed my jeans last night. An otter I saved from a trap yesterday was so scared he peed on me.'

Calum laughed as he imagined the scene. 'Are you sure it was only one otter? It smells like a roomful of skunks here!'

'He must have been really scared,' Josh replied, smiling. His heart was thumping. 'I think it affects their pee.'

'At least your room is relatively tidy,' Calum said. 'But get those jeans in the wash. Now! I don't want the whole house to stink like this.' He chuckled as he retreated down the ladder.

After Josh heard the door to Calum's bedroom close, he rescued Reggae from under the bedclothes. 'That was close,' he whispered. 'We can't leave it any longer. I'll put my jeans in the machine. And then we're going to go out to find you a new home.'

Chapter 5

Josh's school was the only secondary on the island. It was right at the edge of the main town, within easy walking distance for Josh. Many students had to travel a long distance to the school. Most people on the island had to make a special trip to get to town.

It wasn't like the town was huge. Especially in comparison to the city where Josh grew up. But it had everything an islander would need: a pharmacy, post office, several bakers and places to buy clothes and food. Josh knew other people from his school ordered things from the internet, and that people from the south of the island went over the new bridge to the mainland to buy clothes and food. But Calum and Josh bought everything they needed in town. Calum felt it was important to support the local shops.

Because the school was so near the town, a lot of students went into it at lunchtime, or after school, before their buses left for their homes. Josh wasn't one of them. Doing anything in town involved spending money. Money he didn't have, especially now, when he was saving every penny to feed Reggae.

But today he had to buy stuff for Reggae's new home. He'd emptied out his savings, which amounted to less than £2, so he knew he was restricted to the charity shop. But he was optimistic he would find everything he needed there.

Josh stopped at the butcher first. He wanted to see Joanna, the butcher's wife. As he entered the small shop, the wonderful smell of fresh sausages and grass-fed beef hit him. Suddenly, he was starving. Instead of eating lunch, he'd gone home to play with Reggae and change her newspapers.

He spotted Joanna coming out of the big freezer at the back of the shop. She was a big, warm-hearted woman, with lots of freckles and wild red hair that was always escaping from her hairnet.

'Hi Joanna,' he said, pleased to see her. She wasn't always at the shop. She had three kids. And a very time-intensive hobby.

'Josh!' she replied. 'I haven't seen you in ages.' She looked at his empty hands. 'No cubs for me today?'

Calum had introduced Josh to Joanna several years earlier, when Josh had discovered a fox cub whose mother had been killed on the commons. Joanna was well known on the island for saving just such cubs. Over the years, Josh had supplied her with quite a few more. He knew that a lot of crofters didn't approve. They regarded foxes as pests. But Joanna loved foxes.

'Just dropped by to say hello.'

Joanna came out from behind the counter and gave Josh a big, motherly hug. Josh knew better than to struggle. Lifting sides of beef made her incredibly strong. 'That's very nice of you.' Then she held him at arm's length. 'Are you eating enough?'

Josh smiled. Joanna's exuberant personality reminded me of his mum. She was always worried about how much he was eating too.

'I'm not going to starve.'

'That's not good enough,' Joanna declared. She went behind the counter and chose several of Josh's favourite sausages.

'I can't . . .'

'Don't you say another word! These are a gift for you and Calum.' She then emptied a metal bowl of meat scraps into a plastic bag. 'And these are for the wee ones in your care.'

'That's not necessary,' Josh protested. But he thought, Reggae will have a feast tonight.

As Josh headed for the charity shop, he couldn't help thinking about how different Joanna and his mum were from Calum. Their personalities seemed to overflow their bodies, where Calum kept his firmly in check. Sometimes it was hard to believe that Calum and his mum had been brother and sister. His Aunt Gertrude was different again. But, even though she lived on the island, he hardly saw her because she spent so much time on the mainland with her daughter and grandchildren.

In the charity shop, Josh nodded to the older woman who was behind the cash register. She nodded back, then returned to her conversation with a small, grey-haired man Josh didn't recognise.

At the counter, they had a small display of huge

rawhide dog bones. Josh picked one up and fingered it, thinking about how much Reggae would love it. Then he noticed the price, and put it down. He had to be realistic. With £2, he couldn't buy *everything* he wanted.

He went to the back of the store, and searched through the plastic items. He found a large red plastic washing-up bowl that would serve as a bed, and a smaller bowl that Reggae could use as a toilet. The rest of his money went on a couple of old blankets, a tin of dog food, and some cheap dog toys.

Back at the counter, he paid for everything with the change he'd taken from his piggy bank. He carefully packed all his purchases into a large black bin bag. He'd almost finished when the grey-haired man picked up one of the big rawhide bones from the counter and added it to the bin bag.

'My treat,' he said, smiling.

Josh couldn't believe his luck.

* * *

Josh's bedroom was dark, lit only by the bedside lamp. His rucksack was almost full. He turned to look at Reggae, sitting on his bed watching him intently. He wanted to remember what it was like to have her in his room. It had been wonderful having her sleep in the bed with him every night. He would miss her.

Josh put his hand under the fast-growing puppy and lifted her into the air. He flew her around like an aeroplane, making an engine noise, then landed her just inside the rucksack. She looked up at him intently. He put his finger to his mouth and fastened the rucksack over her head.

In a moment, he was down the ladder and in the living room.

'I'm off to the sleepover now,' Josh said.

His uncle put down his newspaper.

'I'm really pleased you've made a friend,' he said earnestly.

A wave of guilt swept over Josh. There wasn't really a friend. A whimper came from his rucksack. Josh coughed loudly to cover it up.

'You're not coming down with a cold?' his uncle worried.

Josh felt Reggae shift her position at the top of the rucksack. 'I'm fine. Got to go,' he said, hurrying towards the door.

'Have a good time!' his uncle shouted after him.

Once they were in the garden, Josh relaxed.

'That was tricky,' he whispered.

He turned on his torch and found the bin bag from the charity shop, which he'd hidden in the bushes at the side of the house. Then he headed towards the far end of the farm. Reggae whimpered again.

'I know it's not comfortable,' Josh said. But we'll be at your new home in a couple of minutes. I hate that you won't be staying with me. But if you're discovered in my room, I might lose you. I can't risk that.'

His torch picked out a tumbledown shed in the

distance. It was situated at the far end of Calum's farm, near a stand of trees that ran down the hill to a river that flowed down from the commons. The whole right side had caved in. It was perfect, from Josh's point of view. No one would suspect this broken-down building was being used as a kennel. And because it was so near the trees, he'd be able to take Reggae out for walks and keep her hidden from prying eyes.

Josh tried the door. It was jammed. He'd noticed this the day before but he hadn't had time to fix it yet. He put his shoulder to it, pulled back and shoved hard. The frame gave way with a loud protest and the door flew open.

He laid the rucksack on the floor and undid the strap. Reggae leapt out. The torch on the floor highlighted her and cast a huge shadow on the wall, making her look as big as a lion. She looked at Josh reproachfully. Josh removed an old oil-burning lantern. He'd found it in the barn where his uncle kept things 'that might be useful some day'. He'd filled it with oil and tested it after school.

It lit first time, and the old shed was filled with a delicate, flickering yellow light. The right side was damp. The sweet smell of slowly rotting wood came from it. But the other half, where Reggae would stay, was dry and waterproof. Josh switched off the torch.

She would be safe here from the island's strong winds, rain and from snow come winter.

Reggae sniffed the lantern. Then she backed away – she'd discovered it was hot. She turned her

31

attention to the earth floor. It seemed to be full of interesting smells.

'I know you're really young to be here on your own,' Josh explained. 'But Borders like you have been bred to be tough. And because the shed's on my way to school, I can see you before I go. Then I'll sneak out at lunch. I can be here in fifteen minutes. That'll give us half an hour together. And after that, it's less than two hours till I'm finished for the day, and I can spend the rest of the afternoon with you.'

Reggae tossed some of the loose hay on the floor into the air with her nose. Then she charged through it as it fell.

'I can tell Uncle Calum I'm going for a walk before bed, so I can tuck you in. It's not great, I know. But it's the best I can do. And of course on the weekends – apart from chores – I'll be with you all the time!'

Josh opened the black bin bag. First, he removed the red plastic washing up bowl. He filled it with the old blankets.

'Your new bed, Madame,' he said, gesturing towards it. Reggae jumped in, and started using her teeth to rearrange the blankets.

Somehow, it reminded Josh of the way his mother would fuss over the duvet as he lay in his bed, adjusting it until it was 'just right'. He closed his eyes to fix the scene in his mind. He was too old for duvet fussing now. But it was nice to remember his mother doing it.

He removed the smaller plastic bowl, then filled it with newspapers from his rucksack.

Satisfied with her bed, Reggae walked over to the bowl. She climbed in and squatted. 'Good girl!' Josh exclaimed. He pulled a treat out of his jeans. Reggae scoffed it.

Finally, Josh removed a sleeping bag from his rucksack. He unrolled it on the floor.

'You didn't think I'd let you spend your first night here alone?'

Having arranged all of Reggae's 'furniture', Josh took out the huge rawhide bone from the bin bag.

Josh stretched out his arm and put the rawhide under Reggae's nose. She sniffed curiously. Then she mouthed it. Josh pulled it away from her, holding it to his chest.

'Mine,' he said. Reggae hardly seemed to think before she jumped up on his lap to get the bone.

'That was quick,' Josh exclaimed.

He let her have one end and they growled at one another. He let her tug it away, and then pulled it back. He loved the way she showed her little teeth and her whole face wrinkled with the effort to win the bone. In the end, he let her 'win', and she paraded around the shed with her prize.

It was starting to get chilly. Josh took off his jeans and shirt and tossed them on the ground. Reggae sniffed around them, and then lay down on his shirt.

Somehow, this reminded Josh of something ... He crawled into his sleeping bag. That was it! His first night on the island. He'd been lying in his new bed. Even though it wasn't that cold, he couldn't stop shivering. Nor could he sleep. In the early hours of the morning, his Aunt Gertrude had come into his room. She'd just been to the city, emptying his mother's flat. She had a bag of his things.

The first thing she'd taken out of the bag was his mother's nightshirt. It still smelled strongly of her. Without a word, she'd put it under his pillow. He hadn't really understood why. A few minutes later, he'd fallen into a dreamless sleep.

He'd forgotten all about that! Funny, how Reggae helped him recall these things.

'I guess tomorrow's going to be like my first night on the island for you.' Josh said thoughtfully. He got out of the sleeping bag, took the blankets from Reggae's bed and lined the sleeping bag with them.

'They'll smell of me tomorrow,' he told her. 'Come on in.'

She climbed onto him, and snuggled into his armpit.

'You won't be able to work with sheep for a while,' Josh said. 'Your body isn't big or strong enough. You'll need to be six months old before we can do anything serious. You're not going to be lying around doing nothing though. You can roam the commons with me. And I'll teach you the usual stuff, "Sit", "Come", "Stay".'

Reggae leaned up and licked Josh's face.

'It usually takes at least two years to train a sheepdog properly,' Josh continued. 'But I'll never be able to keep you secret that long. So I'm going

35

to get you ready to do next summer's Gathering. It won't be easy. The Gathering is a huge test for a dog. Three solid days of hard work, gathering sheep who don't want to be gathered from the commons and bringing them to the pens. The third day is the worst. That's up on the cliffs. Dogs are lost there, because the cliffs crumble underneath them. Then, if we survive that, there's the fank. That's another week of moving the sheep from one pen to another, making sure they all get vaccinated and checked for disease.'

Josh turned off the lantern. 'I've never heard of a one-year-old dog doing it all before . . . But it must be possible.'

Josh felt Reggae shift position to get comfortable. 'I'm sure it's possible,' he said under his breath.

Chapter 6
Five months later

Reggae jumped up and down, almost unable to contain herself. She'd been cooped up in her shed all day. Now that Josh was finally here, she knew she was going out, and she was bursting with energy. He usually came at lunchtime, but a teacher had been patrolling the hole in the school fence that he usually used to sneak away.

Reggae was almost fully grown now. She'd never be a big dog, but she had a big heart.

'Sit,' Josh commanded. Without hesitating, Reggae sat.

Josh attached a lead to her collar. Reggae continued to sit, though she was quivering with excitement. She was waiting for him to release her.

Josh went outside the shed, and inspected the area up the hill, on the other side of the road, where the farmhouses overlooked them. The coast was clear.

He went back inside the shed. 'That'll do.' Reggae jumped up. Josh closed the door behind them. 'Heel.' Reggae fell into step by his side. They headed straight into the strand of trees that ran down the hill towards the loch. Near the loch, at the bottom of the hill, there was a dip that had been carved by the old river, now just a stream. Josh's grandfather had planted birch, alder and mountain ash trees along it, many years ago. Now they were almost fully grown. They provided a place for wildlife.

The trees also hid the two of them as they jogged towards the commons. When the farmhouses were far behind, they headed up the loch side of a steep hill.

Josh had carefully worked out this circuitous route so that they'd be hidden from view. It was a small island; if anybody saw him with a dog, Reggae wouldn't be secret for long.

It started to drizzle. Great. Rain would keep most people off the commons, especially where they were heading today, the round pen.

Josh had found the broken-down pen several years earlier, while he was first exploring the commons. He hadn't understood what it was. But when he'd started puzzling over books about training dogs, he'd discovered that such pens were used to train working dogs – to give them their first experience of working with sheep.

Most farmers had their own pens now, which was why the fence around the one on the commons was falling down. Josh had made repairing it his project for the winter. Every day, with Reggae by his side, he'd carried pieces of wood from his uncle's 'may come in useful' barn all the way here. He'd fixed every gap in the fence.

As they approached the pen, the drizzle turned into a steady rain. At least they didn't have to worry about passers-by. But Josh had a bigger problem.

All the books he'd read had said it was crucial that you were calm and in control the first time you introduced a dog to working with sheep.

But how was he supposed to be calm? He'd never done this before! Okay, he'd watched crofters use dogs to herd sheep. He'd even worked with a few of his uncle's dogs before. But they were old, experienced dogs. He'd never seen anyone *introduce* a dog to working with sheep, except on YouTube. And all the books said if he didn't get this right, it would take months to repair the damage. Josh didn't have months!

Now Reggae had picked up his anxiety and was bouncing up and down, hardly able to contain herself. Somehow, Josh had to get hold of himself. Otherwise all the work he'd done in mending the pen would go to waste.

'Down.' In spite of her excitement and the soaking ground, Reggae lay down. Josh took some comfort from this. He'd trained her well, so far. She knew 'stop' and 'that'll do', and 'down', 'sit' and 'stay'.

Kneeling down next to her, he ran his hand gently along the side of her face. Gradually, Reggae began to relax. The contact with her helped him calm down too.

'I left the gate to the pen open last night,' he told her. 'With any luck, some sheep will have wandered in to eat the fresh grass inside.'

Reggae looked up at him thoughtfully. Josh knew she didn't *really* understand what he was saying,

39

but telling her what they were going to do made it clearer in his mind.

'At first, I'll be in the pen and you'll be outside. You need to learn how your position affects the sheep. If you do well, tomorrow you can come in with me.'

Calmer and more centred, Josh stood and led Reggae over the hill. His plan had worked! There were five sheep and two lambs in the pen.

'Down.' While Reggae lay on her tummy and watched, Josh closed the gate to the pen.

Then he removed a 'long lead' from his rucksack and attached it to her collar. This was a rope five metres long, with knots in it. It would trail after her and if she did something wrong, Josh could jump on it to stop her quickly.

'Up.' Josh led her closer to the pen. About ten metres away, he stopped. 'Sit.' Reggae sat. Her shining eyes were focused on the sheep in the pen. Josh walked slowly to Reggae's left, paying out the lead as he did so.

When he was in front of the gate, Josh stopped. He waited until Reggae looked away from him, to her right. Josh made a 'shushing' noise and Reggae started to run around the pen. As she did, Josh entered the pen, closing the gate behind him.

At first, Reggae just circled the pen again and again. But then she got bored. She began to notice that as she moved, the sheep did too. She stopped. The sheep moved away from her. She moved to her right. The sheep shifted away from her again.

Josh could almost see the moment where Reggae 'got it'. That her job was to move so that the sheep were driven towards Josh.

Josh moved to his left, Reggae to her left, to balance him. Josh moved to his right, and Reggae moved to her right, so that she was opposite him.

'That'll do,' Josh said. He left the pen. That had gone better than he'd expected!

He called Reggae. She saw him reaching into his trouser pocket for a treat, and raced towards him.

Ten minutes later, Josh repeated the whole process. This time, he started off to her right. Instead of circling, Reggae stopped opposite him. When he moved, she did too. She'd got 'lesson one' of learning to be a working dog!

*   *   *

Back in Reggae's shed, Josh hung up his 'work clothes' and changed back into his dry school uniform. Then he opened a tin of dog food. Reggae sat watching him intently. Josh moved over to the wooden box he used as a chair and sat down.

'Go.' Reggae bounded over to the bowl and started to eat.

As she ate, Josh thought about something that had happened two short months ago, when the earliest of the spring lambs were being born. He'd been training Reggae to heel. Some dancing lambs on a neighbouring hill had caught her eye. He didn't have her on the lead and she'd headed for them, ignoring his command to 'stop'. All excited, she'd circled the group of lambs and ewes. Josh had been terrified that Reggae would accidentally hurt one of the lambs. This was a serious matter on the island, and dogs had been shot for this. Fortunately, when the big ewes saw Reggae, they'd started to move towards her. Alarmed, she'd sped back to Josh.

She'd come a long way since then.

'You did really well today,' Josh told her, as she gobbled her food. 'According to the weather forecast, this rotten weather will continue tomorrow. We'll see if you can work *in* the pen. Then you'll really start getting what being a sheepdog is all about.'

Chapter 7

Josh raced across the muddy field, carrying a marga-rine tub and a kitchen roll. After school he'd stopped at home to pick them up, and to change into shorts. That had been a good idea. His legs were already spattered with mud.

The small grove of trees lay just ahead. Josh slowed down. He didn't want to trip. Today's thunderstorm had been especially violent, even by island standards. He'd already found one of its victims.

'What are you doing?' The girl's voice startled Josh. He was crouched under a tree, still breathing heavily from his sprint. Had she *followed* him?

'I asked what *are* you doing?' The voice was impa-tient now. Josh hadn't exactly been ignoring her. It was just that he didn't want to turn away. There wasn't much time to get this right.

Reluctantly, he swung around to face her. He wasn't very good at talking to people. Especially girls.

He recognised her immediately. It was Yvonne, the vet's daughter. She was always getting awards for this and that in the school assemblies. Sometimes she walked home with Kearney. At least *he* wasn't there.

He beckoned her with his hand. Yvonne was still wearing her green school uniform. It made her thin brown hair look dull. She hesitated before leaving the path. But her curiosity won out, and she stepped carefully over the thick blanket of old rotting leaves, twigs and branches.

'Ohhh,' she cooed, when she saw what Josh was cupping in his hands. It was a baby bird he'd found, wet and bedraggled. 'Are you sure you should be doing that? I read that once you get your smell on them their mothers won't feed them.'

'That's rubbish,' Josh said. 'I've saved dozens of birds.' He thought for a moment. 'As long as you're here, you can help. Put your hands together.'

For a moment, Yvonne held back. Then she knelt and stretched out her cupped hands. Gently, he put the bird down in them.

'Keep her warm,' he said. 'Smell isn't a problem. Cold is. Her mother won't feed her if she's cold.'

He speedily laid out layers of kitchen roll in the empty margarine tub. He'd already punched in holes for drainage. 'Put her in. Carefully.'

Yvonne lent over the yellow tub. She opened her hands and the little bird hopped out.

'Why aren't you putting it back in its nest?' she asked quietly.

Josh pointed to the tree above. Yvonne looked up, tilting her glasses to see better. The remains of the nest were just barely visible.

'The thunderstorm this afternoon,' he explained.

He used his arms to grasp hold of a branch above him. Pulling himself off the ground, he wrapped his legs around the tree.

'Here,' he said. Yvonne put the tub in his outstretched hand. Keeping the hand holding the tub free, Josh began to climb. He wedged the tub into a group of small branches, then shook the main bough gently to make sure it would stay put. Then, using both hands, he climbed down.

Yvonne watched him in silence. 'You're strong!'

Josh had never thought of himself as strong, though he did the work of an adult on the farm. He pointed towards an old oak. 'We can watch.' He led the way.

They could hear the baby blackbird's distressed 'cheep, cheep'. Yvonne shifted from foot to foot, her forehead wrinkled with worry. 'Will the mother come?'

Josh put his finger to his mouth and kept his eyes on the yellow tub.

After what seemed like ages, a brown female bird flew onto the branch above the makeshift nest. She inspected the tub. Then she hopped down and stood on its side. She lent over, and they could see her regurgitate a worm. It disappeared into the baby bird's mouth.

Josh glanced at Yvonne, suddenly worried she might be upset at the sight. But Yvonne was unmoved. Josh remembered seeing her driving around in the vet's brightly painted van with him, probably doing rounds. She'd probably seen a lot worse that a bird vomiting up worms . . .

He smiled, pleased at figuring this out, and at having another successful rescue under his belt. But suddenly, he felt awkward. He didn't know what to say to Yvonne.

'I've got chores,' he told her. And without another word, he ran off.

He caught a glimpse of Yvonne – her mouth was open and her eyes wide, as if she'd been shocked by something. Not him, surely . . .

* * *

As they ran along the old river, the light rain continued.

'I saved a bird today,' Josh told Reggae. 'And this girl from my class helped.' Reggae looked up at Josh. 'I think it went okay.'

It started to rain in earnest. Josh examined the sky, a heavy grey in all directions.

'It's settling in,' he said. 'Let's see what you remember back at the pen.'

Chapter 8

The following day after school, Josh returned to the woods to see how the baby bird was doing. As he approached the oak where he and Yvonne had hidden the previous day, he was surprised to see a glimpse of a school uniform. Someone was already there. He approached quietly.

'Oh!' Yvonne exclaimed. 'I didn't hear you coming! I ran all the way here because I wanted to see how our bird was doing!'

'It's not *our* bird,' Josh snapped. 'It's mine.' It was! The fourth he'd rescued this spring!

Yvonne reacted sharply. '*My* bird, *my* bird,' she said imitating him and sounding like a three-year-old.

Josh blushed.

'I thought you were different,' Yvonne said, now sounding hurt and turning away from him.

Josh didn't understand. How could she be angry and hurt at the same time? And what did she mean when she said she'd thought he was different? They'd barely exchanged a word before yesterday. Surely she'd never given him a moment's thought . . .

'I'm not different,' he said.

Yvonne didn't turn towards him to speak. 'You feed the school rabbit and guinea pig when the teacher forgets. You tickle their tummies when you think no one's looking. And you told that support teacher off when he pulled the rabbit's ear too hard. That was really brave!'

'I didn't think . . . anyone noticed,' Josh said quietly. He always felt invisible at school. Unless he was being told off.

'Well, you were wrong,' Yvonne said, still facing away.

Josh thought a moment. 'Maybe I was wrong about the bird too,' he said softly. 'You *did* help me rescue her.'

Yvonne turned to face him. 'Do you mean it?'

Josh nodded. 'I'm just used . . . to doing things by myself.'

Yvonne pointed to the tub nest. 'The mother comes every couple of minutes to feed her.'

After a few minutes, Josh said, 'It's not just the mother. It's the father too. He's the black one with the yellow beak. There!'

Yvonne kept her eye on the nest. 'You're right! You know a lot about birds.'

'I spend a lot of time watching them,' Josh said. 'You have to if you want to give them what they need.'

'You're good at that?' Yvonne asked.

'With animals,' Josh admitted. 'I'm not very good at figuring out people.'

Yvonne smiled, as if she knew what Josh was talking about. 'What will happen to the fledgling?'

'She'll be ready to leave the nest soon,' Josh said.

'Oh,' Yvonne said, disappointed.

'She'll still be there tomorrow,' Josh reassured her.

'Can I come and watch her after school?' Yvonne asked. Her voice had become almost inaudible.

'Of course,' Josh said. 'She's your bird too!'

Yvonne gave him a shy smile. For a brief moment, Josh had a wild, unreasonable thought: Maybe this girl could become his friend. But then he pushed it out of his mind.

* * *

The next day, as usual, Josh had rushed back to Reggae's shed to spend time with her at lunchtime. But he'd returned to school early, because he had to try to look up his English homework on the computer in the library. They didn't have one at home.

He didn't notice Yvonne until she sat down next to him. 'You weren't at lunch,' she said. 'Aren't you hungry?'

Josh was starving. But he shook his head. And hurriedly pressed the minimise icon on the screen. He didn't want Yvonne to see the Help page he was looking at.

But he was too late. '*I* can help you with English,' Yvonne said. She added quickly, 'If you want.'

Josh shook his head. If Yvonne realised how thick he was, she'd never talk to him again.

Luckily, Yvonne switched the subject. 'You used to have lunch all the time. Six months ago you stopped. Why?'

Josh didn't know what to say. He skipped lunch

because he needed the money for dog food. But he *couldn't* tell her that . . .

'It's hard to explain.'

Yvonne suddenly seemed very interested in the way the librarian was putting books onto the shelves. Had he been too sharp?

'Honest, it's not you,' Josh added quickly.

Yvonne turned back to him and nodded slightly.

Josh had a thought and, after a moment, decided to chance saying it out loud.

'Would you like to come to see our bird with me after school?'

Yvonne smiled.

* * *

Two days later, the baby bird was standing on the side of the tub now, stretching her wings.

'Isn't it lovely?' Yvonne said. 'Just think: she wouldn't be there if we hadn't rescued her!'

For a moment, Josh was annoyed at the 'we'. But he had to admit it had been fun watching the bird with Yvonne over the last couple of days. She'd even walked with him here today – that made it two days in a row. He'd miss all this now that the fledgling was about to fly its nest.

'About lunch,' he said. 'I skip it on purpose. But you mustn't tell anyone.'

'I can keep a secret,' Yvonne said firmly.

Josh believed her. He couldn't figure out her moods but he'd noticed something about her the

52

last couple of days. He'd always thought of her as someone who talked with everyone and who had lots of friends. But actually, she spent most of her time alone, watching other people. Like him.

'It's just I need the money my uncle gives me for lunch. For something else.'

Yvonne didn't say anything. She just continued looking at the baby blackbird. Josh was pleased she wasn't pressing him to say something.

Did he really want to share his big secret? She might laugh, or even worse, tell. But if he didn't take a risk now, he might never have the chance to talk to her again.

Josh made a decision. He bent down and opened his school bag. 'I buy this with it,' he said quietly, holding up two tins.

'You have a dog?' Yvonne said in a hushed voice. 'A secret dog?'

Chapter 9

The valley that Josh had chosen for training Reggae was as secret as Josh could find. It was surrounded by steep hills and it was off the usual walking routes on the commons.

As Josh led Reggae up the hill towards it, he remembered the envelope in his school jacket. He shook his head. He didn't need to think about his school report until later. He had more important things to deal with.

He was going to start to work with Reggae in the open.

It had taken ten days to teach Reggae everything he could in the pen. It had been a real struggle rebuilding it over the winter. But it had been worth it to give Reggae a good first experience of working with sheep.

The fencing of the pen was like a safety net for a trapeze artist. Now they'd have to do without it. Many young dogs found working with sheep in the open just too exciting. They raced around, scaring ewes and lambs. If he and Reggae didn't work well together, the sheep would run away or even worse, hurt themselves on the uneven ground of the commons. If a single lamb was hurt, he, and more importantly, Reggae, would be in serious trouble.

But there was no help for it. The Gathering was less than two months away. Usually it took more than a year of working a dog to prepare for it. They had no time to waste.

*   *   *

As they came over the hill, Josh saw that there was a group of eight sheep grazing near the bottom of the valley. Perfect.

'Stop,' Josh said firmly. Reggae stopped, though her eyes were focused on the sheep below. Josh attached a long lead, which would trail after Reggae as she ran. Josh knew sheep are much more relaxed about a dog on a lead than one running free.

Josh led Reggae down the hill.

'Heel.'

He walked closer to the sheep. Then, about ten metres away, he stopped. Still looking towards the sheep, he commanded, 'Away.'

He'd taught Reggae this command in the pen. Would she remember what it meant?

Reggae started off to her right, then circled behind the sheep. She was keeping a good distance, Josh observed. The sheep weren't spooked. Josh moved to his left, keeping the same distance from the sheep. Reggae moved so that she was opposite him.

The biggest ewe suddenly noticed Reggae. She started to move towards her. Reggae retreated and barked once. But the big sheep kept going, picking up speed as she went. Reggae went low and growled

56

loudly. But the ewe didn't stop. The rest of the group was following. Oh no! Why did they have to get such an aggressive sheep on their first run? Reggae would be trampled if she wasn't careful!

Reggae backed off again and barked several times. But the big ewe wasn't going to stop for this noisy small dog. Reggae's ears and tail went up. Josh knew that meant she was about to do something. But what?

She leapt into the air and towards the fast-approaching ewe. And then, in mid-air, Reggae twisted her body and fastened her mouth onto the sheep's nose. Josh held his breath. *What* was she doing?

The ewe shook the dog from side to side. But Reggae wouldn't let go. The big ewe stopped. Immediately, Reggae released her grip and backed off about five metres. She just stood there with her eyes fixed on the ewe. Josh realised that she had only held on a couple of seconds, even though it had *seemed* like much longer.

The now wary ewe stood too, her flock behind her. Clearly she had underestimated this dog. But Reggae wasn't barking or being aggressive. Indeed, she just stood there, eyes alert. Josh saw the ewe's posture change, from challenging to calm. Reggae stayed alert, and her eyes glanced sideways.

Josh could hardly believe what he'd just witnessed. Reggae had known exactly what she needed to do to turn the threatening situation around!

'Come by,' he commanded.

Reggae took a small step to her left. The big ewe took note, then began to turn. Her flock followed. Josh circled to his left so his dog was directly opposite.

Reggae crept forward. One of the lambs started to dance away from her mother. Reggae immediately moved a few steps to the lamb's right, to stop her from getting away. Josh's heart swelled with pride. He clicked approvingly. He'd heard men talk about natural dogs but he'd never seen one before.

Reggae took a step forward. The big ewe lifted her head. Keeping low, Reggae crept forward again.

'Away.'

Reggae crept to her right, and then forward again, her ears flat against her head. When a skittish lamb started to leave the flock, she quickly moved to her left and the big ewe and her group of sheep moved towards Josh.

This was the crucial time. Once the group started moving, any one of them could head off in another direction. Josh and Reggae had to keep them together. Another ewe started off to the left. Reggae immediately backed up and circled to her left, still crouching, ready for action. The ewe rejoined the group.

Together, they manoeuvred the group towards Josh. When they were just a metre away, Josh said, 'That'll do.' He walked backwards. Reggae retreated too.

The group of sheep relaxed and started to graze.

'Come,' Josh ordered. He stroked Reggae's cheek. Reggae closed her eyes with pleasure. Then she rolled onto the ground and Josh rubbed her tummy. 'That was brilliant. You're brilliant!'

They repeated the process once more. This time, it went more smoothly. From the books Josh had read, he knew he mustn't work her too long this early in her training. Anyway, he had chores to do at home.

'Kennel,' he said. Reggae just sat there, avoiding Josh's eyes and staring in the direction of the sheep. She wanted to keep working. Josh didn't repeat himself; he knew that would just teach Reggae it was okay not to obey the first time he gave a command. He simply got up and started to jog towards home. Reggae followed immediately.

* * *

As Reggae noisily consumed her dinner that evening, Josh said, 'I have to admit that when I saw you bite that ewe's nose, I thought you'd lost it. But it was exactly the right thing! And you released her as soon as she got the message. I guess if you're a wee dog you've got to have ways to make the sheep listen.'

Reggae was finished and came over for a stroke. Josh bent over and blew into her ear. Reggae licked his face. 'That big ewe could've trampled you.'

Suddenly, Josh recalled his mother singing. 'The harder they come, the harder they fall . . .' Her lilting, slightly out-of-tune voice came back to him. He couldn't remember who sang the song. He looked at

Reggae, surprised. Once again, she'd brought back memories of his mum.

Josh embraced the black and white dog. It was starting to get dark beyond the shed door.

It was then that he remembered the envelope in his rucksack. The one containing his school report. It was sealed and he hadn't bothered opening it. He knew what was inside. Bad news. His uncle wouldn't be happy.

'I've got to go,' he said. 'I'll be back later, to say goodnight.'

Under his breath, Josh added, 'I hope.'

Chapter 10

Josh scrubbed the carrots in the sink with the worn bristle brush. They were uneven and gnarled. He didn't know how they got the ones in the Co-op in the town so straight. One out of ten from their garden looked like that. Surely they didn't throw the rest away . . .

Without thinking, he whistled. After a moment he recognised the tune. It was 'The Harder They Come'. He smiled to himself.

He started chopping the now (relatively) clean carrots. His uncle came into the kitchen, wearing a clean shirt and trousers, his hair still wet from a freezing cold shower. His uncle thought these showers helped you avoid colds. He was a pretty good advertisement for this theory. He'd only been ill once in the five years Josh had known him.

'What's left to do?' Calum asked.

'We just need to clean and steam the broccoli,' Josh replied. 'I'll cook the lamb steaks.'

Calum nodded, went to the vegetable larder and pulled out a large head of broccoli. It did well on the island, so they ate quite a lot of it. Fortunately, Josh had grown to like it.

'Broccoli's very good for you,' his uncle remarked as he put it under the cold tap to clean it.

'Really?' Josh replied. His uncle told him this almost every time they ate it, roughly a hundred times a year . . . He moved to the Aga, pulled down a frying pan, and added some oil to it. As it warmed, he went to the meat fridge and pulled out some lamb steaks.

The steaks, broccoli and carrots were ready more or less at the same time. Josh took out a couple of large plates from one of the dark cupboards, and put a steak on each. Calum added the vegetables, while Josh removed a couple of baked potatoes from inside the Aga's oven. A feast. Calum liked having a special meal on Friday night.

But Josh had a feeling he wasn't going to enjoy it much.

*　　*　　*

They sat at the small round dining table in silence as usual. The envelope seemed be growing in the rear pocket of Josh's jeans. He'd fluffed the chance to give it to his uncle before his shower.

Now he had to wait until the meal was finished. And his uncle would be angry not only about what was in the report but also the delay in giving it to him. But as the fresh butter from his cousin's farm melted onto the floury Maris Piper he'd collected earlier from the potato store in the cellar, the smell of the food and his hunger helped him put the envelope out of his mind.

As he watched his uncle mopping up the remaining

gravy on his now empty plate Josh knew he couldn't put it off any longer. He pulled the now heavily crumpled envelope from his back pocket and handed it to his uncle. His hand shook. As soon as his uncle took the envelope, Josh pulled his hand away and sat on it.

His uncle's nose wrinkled at the sight of the scrunched-up envelope.

'You should have taken better care of this. It's from the school,' he said, as he got up to search the sideboard for his reading glasses. When he found them, he went to his writing desk and found the paper knife he'd inherited from Josh's grandfather. He came back to the kitchen table, sat down, and slit the envelope open. His big hands carefully took the paper from inside and unfolded it.

Josh had forced himself to keep breathing as his uncle searched for his glasses, then the paper knife. But now the moment of truth had come. His uncle took his time reading (and probably re-reading) the report. Then he got up, went to the writing desk and pulled out Josh's last report. He brought it back to the table, and put them side by side. He took his time comparing the two.

Finally, after what seemed like an eternity, he looked up at Josh. His eyes were full of disappointment. 'Is something wrong at school?'

Josh shook his head.

His uncle looked at him steadily. 'Your attendance has been good.' Josh knew he must have searched for something positive to say. 'But, your work in English,

history and maths are still unsatisfactory. And your expected level of achievement has gone down, rather than up in the most important subjects.'

Josh knew all this. What he didn't know, and was waiting to find out, was what his uncle proposed to do about this.

'We've talked about this before,' his uncle began. 'If you don't get better grades, you'll never have any choices in life. I didn't do well at school and when I was eighteen all I could do was work on my father's croft.'

This didn't seem so bad to Josh. He liked their life, though it was hard work at times.

'You have to improve these grades,' his uncle continued. 'Which means you'll have to spend less time on the commons. Until your grades improve, you'll need to come home after school and study.'

Involuntarily, Josh drew in a deep breath. If he wasn't allowed to go on the commons, he couldn't complete Reggae's training. And if he couldn't complete her training he couldn't participate in the Gathering and Reggae would have to stay secret another year!

He absolutely couldn't let Calum continue in this line of thinking!

'That won't be necessary,' Josh said, with a calmness he didn't feel, 'Yvonne, the vet's daughter, has agreed to tutor me in maths and English.'

Josh's uncle tilted his head. 'Yvonne? I've heard she's very clever.'

'She's the best in my classes,' Josh agreed.

Suddenly, Uncle Calum became suspicious. 'You haven't mentioned Yvonne before . . .'

'She helped me rescue a bird a while ago,' Josh replied. He searched frantically through his mind for what he knew about Yvonne's schedule. 'She can tutor me after school one day a week, and another I can go to her house before dinner.'

'You've already discussed this?' Calum asked.

'Absolutely,' Josh lied. Reggae's future was at stake.

'Won't we have to pay her?'

'She offered to help. She could see I was having trouble with the Shakespeare play we're doing.'

Uncle Calum hesitated. 'I don't see how she'll have time for all this. I often see her out with her father doing his rounds. I'll have a word with him. I'll see him next Wednesday at the Forestry Trust meeting. If it's all right with him, then we'll see if this is enough to improve your grades. But if it doesn't, you'll have to stay in after school. I'll write to the school to ask for them to give you extra homework.'

Josh didn't see that why it was necessary to go *that* far. But he said, 'That's fair. I'm sure it will make a difference.'

He'd have to ask Yvonne before Wednesday. He was pretty confident she'd agree to tutor him. But even if she did, he wasn't sure anything could help him at school.

But at least this bought him enough time to finish Reggae's training. Which was all that mattered.

'I'll tidy up,' Josh said.

'Are you sure? It's my turn.'

'You read the paper.'

Josh cleared the table and set to work washing up. His uncle retired to his favourite armchair. Josh scraped the leftovers into a bowl and then added the water from the vegetables and the fat from the lamb steaks. This would make a special treat for Reggae tomorrow morning. This was why he didn't mind doing more than his share of tidying.

'What's that?' Calum's voice cut into his reverie. He'd come into the kitchen with his empty mug.

'Leftovers.'

'I can *see* that. Why are you collecting them?'

Josh hesitated for a moment. A half-truth, he thought.

'It's for a wounded animal I've rescued,' he said.

'I've seen you coming out of the shed at the far end of the field, near the woods. Do you keep them there?'

Josh's knees almost gave way. His uncle *had* noticed him going to the shed. He willed his voice to stay steady. 'I've fitted it out as a field hospital.'

Calum chuckled and said warmly. 'A field hospital. I should have guessed.'

He handed him the mug and returned to the kitchen. Josh tried to get control of his breathing. He'd done the best he could under the circumstances. He didn't like lying to Calum. But he – and Reggae – were now in greater danger of discovery. Calum could drop by any time to see the animals in the 'field hospital'. He had to say something. Now.

'Uncle Calum,' he said hesitantly. 'I keep a lot of

my stuff in the field hospital. Would you mind if I kept it just for me?'

Josh felt guilty as a hurt look passed across his uncle's face.

'I guess you're becoming a "teenager",' he said thoughtfully. 'And you need your own space . . . Okay. The shed's yours. I wasn't using it anyway.'

'Thank you,' Josh said, meaning it.

Sometimes Calum surprised him

Chapter 11

The following Monday Josh led Yvonne up the wooded path which ended near Reggae's secret kennel. Yvonne had been asking to meet her for some time. It wasn't exactly that Josh didn't want her to – he did ... But he didn't feel Reggae was *ready*. At least until last week. That's when he'd agreed to introduce Yvonne to Reggae. All that was fine. What wasn't fine was that his mouth seemed to have taken on a life of its own. He just couldn't seem to stop talking.

'I know she's really small. But I've trained her to do a lot of things. Some things she just figured out by herself. I don't mean she really figured it out. It happened too fast for that but she just seemed to have an instinct as if she'd read a book about it or been a sheepdog before ...'

As he and Yvonne approached Reggae's shed, he heard himself talking even faster, if that were possible.

'It doesn't look like much but it's really comfortable inside and actually the way it looks on the outside helps because it means no one would guess it's a kennel for a dog.'

To Josh's immense relief Yvonne, who had been silent most of the way from the school, interrupted his torrent of words. 'It's wonderful! Even better than I imagined.'

Better than she'd imagined? It was a wreck! How could she have dreamt up a worse wreck?

Suddenly a terrible thought hit him. What if Yvonne didn't like Reggae?

They arrived at the shed's door. He could hear Reggae scratching.

'I can't wait to meet her,' Yvonne said.

The noise from inside the shed stopped. At first Josh couldn't understand. Then he realised Reggae must have heard Yvonne's voice, and had gone into stealth mode.

'It's okay, girl,' Josh said, speaking to the closed door. But the shed remained silent. He opened the padlock, then the door. They entered. Where was Reggae? She usually jumped on him as soon as he came in.

He closed the door behind them. As his eyes got used to the dim light in the shed, he saw a shadow in the dark, wet corner of the part of the shed that leaked. What was she doing there?

'It's only me,' Yvonne said, quietly.

'You're the first person she's met, apart from me,' Josh said. 'I guess I need to make a formal introduction.'

He was pleased when Yvonne giggled.

Josh slowly approached Reggae in the corner. Yvonne followed his lead. Josh spoke softly. 'Good girl. Well done.' He knelt down and tickled her under her ear. She began to relax.

'This is Yvonne. I brought her to meet you. She's my friend.'

Yvonne smiled shyly at Josh.

Then Reggae got up and walked over to Yvonne. She licked her hand several times. Yvonne gently rubbed the dog's forehead.

'She likes me!' Yvonne said.

'She really does,' Josh agreed.

*　*　*

'Have I told you about our valley?' he asked, as they walked along the old river. Yvonne shook her head. He continued, 'I call it the secret valley, because unless you're on one of the hills that overlook it, you'd never see us training.'

Reggae tugged on the lead, looking at Josh reproachfully. Josh ignored her. So what if he usually let Reggae go here? He was hardly going to jog along with Yvonne.

He continued to talk with her. Reggae pulled on the lead again. Josh stopped, stared at her sternly, and said, 'Heel.' Then he turned back to Yvonne.

There was a different group of sheep in the valley today. A larger group, twelve lambs and ewes. A new challenge for Reggae.

Reggae seemed unusually subdued as he unfastened her lead. Usually she had her eye on the sheep and was itching to go. But instead she kept looking from Josh to Yvonne, and then back again.

'Are you all right?' asked Josh, suddenly concerned. When had Reggae got so out of sorts?

73

After a long glance at Yvonne, Reggae shifted her head to stare at the group of sheep. Josh hoped that meant she was all right.

'Okay,' he urged. 'Let's show Yvonne what we can do. Heel.'

He walked towards the sheep with Reggae by his side. When he glanced back at Yvonne, Reggae looked towards her too, then back at the sheep uncertainly. Josh stopped. He glanced back again and then looked at Reggae. 'Away.'

Reggae looked at Yvonne, then the sheep. She hesitated. Then she started off to his right. Josh circled slowly to his left, then he stopped.

What was Reggae doing? She hadn't stopped opposite him. Instead, she was continuing towards him, making a full circle of the sheep. 'Down,' Josh yelled. But Reggae didn't go down. Instead, she ran past him on her way to do another circuit. Blood rushed to Josh's face. He couldn't believe Reggae was doing this in front of Yvonne!

Reggae continued circling the sheep. This time, as she approached Josh, he moved sideways, with his arms outstretched, to block her path. She simply reversed direction and started to go around the other way.

Josh thought quickly. He could make this work! When she got halfway around the sheep, he moved swiftly to block her path again. Reggae, seeing this, hesitated at the far side of the sheep.

'Down,' Josh commanded firmly. This time Reggae went flat on the ground, more or less opposite Josh.

Okay, this wasn't the way he'd wanted it to look,

but at least Reggae was now in position. Now he had to get her to bring the sheep to him.

He walked backwards, so that Reggae would see she had a job to do. 'Up,' he shouted and gestured. Reggae, who now gave Josh her full attention, stood.

'Come by,' Josh commanded.

Reggae crouched down low and took a few steps to her left. Josh moved a few steps to the left, and Reggae balanced him by moving to the right. She then crept forward, retreating swiftly to the right to urge a lamb that was starting to stray back into position. Soon, the little flock had been brought to Josh.

'That'll do,' Josh said, releasing Reggae.

Josh waited for her to come around and the two of them rejoined Yvonne.

'That was incredible,' Yvonne said. 'And it was only your fourth day working in the open?'

'It was a disaster!' Josh said. 'She should know that she stops opposite me. I don't know what got into her.'

'Lots of young dogs circle the sheep like that,' Yvonne said.

'That's the point,' Josh said. '*Young* dogs do that. Reggae has to act like an old dog. She can't circle the sheep during the Gathering. They won't keep us for a second day.'

'She *is* a young dog,' Yvonne said. 'I know you're in a rush to train her but you mustn't forget that. What matters is not that she circled but that you figured out a way to make it work for you. And that she responded to you.'

Josh looked at Yvonne gratefully. Why didn't his teachers encourage him like she did?

'Do you mind if we do another run?' Josh asked.

'I could watch Reggae all day,' Yvonne said.

* * *

As they walked along the river bed on the way home, Josh remembered the conversation with his uncle. He had to ask Yvonne about tutoring. Now. Then he spotted two people coming towards them round the bend of the river. It was too late for them to hide Reggae. What could they do?

'Psst,' he whispered, nodding his head towards the walkers.

Yvonne glanced up, clocked the walkers and hesitated for a moment. Then she took Reggae's lead smoothly out of his hand. She pulled Reggae towards her and continued to walk towards the man and woman, as if this were the most natural thing in the world.

'Hi, Mr and Mrs MacLeish,' she called, when they were near enough to hear her.

'Tush, Yvonne!' the female walker said. 'It's Karen and John . . . What are you doing here?' The woman looked at Josh, then nodded slightly, as if her question had been answered.

'Josh,' Yvonne said brightly, 'I'd like you to meet Mr . . . Karen and John.'

Josh extended his hand and John shook it warmly.

'The MacLeishes own a croft on the other side

of the loch, just near the sea,' Yvonne explained to Josh.

Without a break, she turned to the MacLeish's. 'How's your calf?'

'She's fine now, thanks to you and your father,' John said

'That girl of yours,' said Karen to Josh, 'is a wonder with animals. Her father would be lost without her.'

Josh glanced at Reggae, who was sitting attentively at Yvonne's side, just as if she belonged to her. Josh thought he should explain to Mrs MacLeish that Yvonne wasn't 'his girl', but before he could get a word out, Yvonne was saying:

'Josh is good with animals too. He was helping me work with one of my father's dogs.'

Karen smiled. Then she really looked at Josh, as if trying to place him.

'I'm Calum McCrae's nephew,' Josh filled in.

'We've got to be going,' Yvonne urged Josh. 'Come on, Spike.' Reggae hesitated for a moment, then stood.

'Remember us to your father,' John said. 'Tell him we hope we won't be needing to see him soon,' he laughed.

Yvonne pulled Reggae along behind her as the couple headed off.

'That was quick thinking,' Josh whispered. 'You should be an actress!'

Yvonne laughed. 'It was lucky Reggae played along . . .'

Josh remembered what he'd been about to do

before the MacLeishes came along. 'Yvonne,' he began. Yvonne looked at him warily.

'Usually sentences that begin with my name end with me being told off.' she said.

'That's not it!' Josh snapped.

Involuntarily, Yvonne stepped back from him.

Josh took a deep breath. 'Sorry. I'm not good at this. Asking for help . . .'

Yvonne's face relaxed. 'You're not going to tell me off?'

'Why would I do that?' Josh said. 'No one's ever been nicer to me!'

'Then why . . .' Yvonne asked, confused.

'I can't help it. I'm rubbish with people.'

'Rubbish, yes,' Yvonne agreed. 'Helpless, no.'

'I'm trying to help it!'

Yvonne sighed. They started walking again. After a bit, she spoke. 'Why don't you start again?'

'Okay.' Josh looked at her mischievously. 'Yvonne . . .' he started.

Yvonne started to giggle. 'By Jove, I think he's got it!'

Now Josh was confused. 'Who's Jove?'

Yvonne touched his arm lightly. 'It's not important. It's a line from one of my mum's favourite movies.'

Josh decided to let this go. He took a deep breath. 'I need help in English, history and maths.'

'I offered to help with English before.'

'I was too stubborn then.'

'Now?'

'My uncle says if I don't improve my grades I can't go on the commons after school.'

Yvonne looked at him, concerned. 'You couldn't finish Reggae's training.'

Josh nodded. 'Could we do two lessons a week?'

'That's a lot.'

'The thing is, I've already told my uncle you've agreed.'

Yvonne punched him on the arm. Hard. She wagged her finger at him. 'Josh McCrae.'

'Uh, oh. Trouble on the way,' Josh said, ducking as if something had been thrown at him.

Yvonne started to laugh. 'You know, you're not as rubbish at people as you think . . .'

Chapter 12

One good thing about racing home every lunch hour to see Reggae, Josh thought, as he arrived back at the school library, was that he was in the best shape ever. He didn't even get winded when he ran back to school.

He wasn't out of breath, but he *was* tired. The night before he'd been up until three trying to figure out why Reggae had misbehaved when he'd been training her with Yvonne. Which really amounted to finding out what Josh had done wrong, as all the training books at the library agreed if your dog had a problem, it was your fault.

He finally decided that he'd come back to school early and look for a solution on the web. He often spent the last ten minutes of his lunch break at a library computer. He'd discovered the internet was a wonderful source of information about training Border collies. There were websites, videos on YouTube and special forums devoted to showing, explaining and even arguing about the best way to teach a working dog.

And Yvonne usually showed up before the end of the lunch break so they could walk to their next classes together. Sometimes, she'd even bring a sandwich.

He googled 'dogs circling sheep' and then clicked on a video on the Border Collie Boards forum.

A harsh voice interrupted his concentration. Josh looked up. It was Kearney and his troll-like sidekick, Angus. Kearney looked at him as if he were a dog that had done a very clever trick. 'You can work a computer?' Then he noticed what Josh was watching. 'Getting a dog are you?'

'My uncle promised he'd get me one if we had a good year,' Josh lied.

'That old miser?' said Kearney, laughing. The librarian gave him a sharp look and he lowered his voice. 'You'll be waiting a long time, City Boy.'

'City Boy,' Angus repeated, chuckling. Angus thought pretty much everything Kearney did was clever. Even a remark that had been old five years earlier.

'I've got a dog,' Kearney bragged. 'A working dog.'

Josh was interested in spite of his dislike for Kearney. 'Really? What kind?'

'It's a Border. It's black with a round white circle around his left eye. My dad gave him to me. I'm training him up.'

'I bet that's difficult,' Josh sympathised.

'Are you joking?' Kearney said. 'It's easy peasy. He'll beat your imaginary dog any day.'

On cue, Angus repeated Kearney's joke. 'Imaginary dog. Good one, Kearney.'

Josh found it difficult to imagine Kearney having the patience to train a dog. Especially him finding it 'easy peasy'.

'I'd like to see him sometime,' he said.

Kearney rolled his eyes, as if Josh had suggested something far too ridiculous to consider. He and Angus left the library. Josh went back to his video, determined that Reggae would be ten times better than any dog Kearney owned and trained.

Josh heard the library door open and automatically checked to see if it was Yvonne. No. Disappointed, he turned back to the computer.

* * *

Josh's next class was citizenship. It was boring, but at least the teacher didn't call on him very often. She only paid attention to the smart kids who asked and answered questions. As he rushed through the hall, he caught sight of Yvonne's stringy brown hair. There she is, he thought, pleased to see her. He was just about to shout out her name when he realised she wasn't on her own. Eric, a tall blond boy who always had his hand up in class, was with her.

They were deep in conversation. Josh felt a bit like he'd stepped into a rabbit hole on the commons – his whole body seemed to be suspended in mid-air before gravity took hold of him.

That was why she hadn't come to see him in the library. She was in the middle of a brilliant conversation with Eric, probably talking about something he couldn't understand. Instantly, Josh reversed direction. He took the other stairs up to the classroom.

His stomach still seemed to be floating, as if the hole he'd stepped into was a lot deeper than he'd expected.

Josh sat staring at the page in his textbook. His mind went back to Yvonne. So she'd found something better to do during lunch. It didn't necessarily *mean* anything.

Then he pictured how absorbed she was in the conversation with Eric. He felt a sharp pang of feeling. Something he hadn't felt for years. The last time was when he'd brought a friend home from school and his mother had been chatting away with him. Jealousy.

He shouldn't kid himself. Yvonne had decided she didn't want to be friends with him. It must have been the fiasco with Reggae the day before . . .

And then he'd asked her to tutor him. *Twice a week!* Josh closed his eyes with embarrassment at the memory. He was glad Yvonne wasn't in citizenship. He didn't have to look at her. And as it was the last class in the day, he could just go straight home afterwards. At least Reggae would be there for him.

*   *   *

'Heel,' Josh said firmly. Reggae fell into step beside him. Josh started to jog. There was nothing better than running after being cooped up in a classroom all day. He couldn't imagine life without the commons. Immediately, Josh felt guilty. If his mother hadn't died, he'd still be living in the city. He stumbled but managed to recover his footing. He had to forget about Yvonne and concentrate on the job at hand. He had a dog to train. Today it was long outruns.

As they neared their valley, he could see Reggae's ears perk up. He knelt down next to her and tickled her under her ear. 'Today it's outruns,' he explained. 'An outrun is when you go off to your right or left to get behind some sheep. You've been doing short ones so far. But in the Gathering, the sheep will be so far away they may be invisible behind a hill or rocky outcrop. I'll have to trust you to get behind the sheep, keep a good distance, and then bring the sheep to me. Okay?'

Josh knew Reggae couldn't understand what he was saying. But *he* found it useful to tell her his goals for the day ahead – it helped him to focus on the job at hand. He suddenly realised he hadn't done this the day before. He'd been too distracted by wanting to impress Yvonne to chat with Reggae.

Suddenly a whole number of images came together in Josh's head. He remembered Reggae tugging on her lead as he walked with Yvonne. Twice. She'd missed running with him to the valley. Just like he'd missed Yvonne at lunch. That's why Reggae had kept looking from him to Yvonne before circling the sheep! She was jealous.

He felt Reggae licking his hand, and Josh realised she was trying to get his attention. He'd been staring into space.

'Sorry, pup,' he said, tickling her under the ear.

'I was just figuring something out. We'll do your outruns now.'

*　*　*

As they ran across the commons together, Josh reflected happily on the afternoon's work. Reggae had really got the idea of outruns. And *he'd* figured out why she'd misbehaved the day before.

Suddenly, ahead of him, he saw a crofter out with his dog on the path that intersected the one they were on. Josh dived to the ground. 'Down, Reggae!' he whispered urgently. Reggae stopped in her tracks and went down on her stomach.

Josh was pretty sure they hadn't been seen, but just in case, he stayed down for at least a minute. Then he lifted his head to check what was happening. He was relieved to see that the crofter had continued on his way. But his dog was another matter. He started running towards Josh, barking frantically. Josh ducked and after a few tense moments, heard the crofter call, 'That'll do, Jay. No time for chasing rabbits. We'll miss dinner.' The dog's barking continued, but now at a greater distance. By listening carefully, Josh could keep track of the crofter's progress. After a couple of minutes, he lifted his head again. He could see that in a few moments, the crofter and his dog would pass over the next rise.

Josh left it a while after they disappeared before standing. This kind of thing was happening more frequently now, as the weather got better. He had to stay alert all the time.

They started again on their way. A few minutes later, Reggae suddenly veered away from his side and started to run towards a gorge on their left.

'We're not home yet,' Josh shouted at her.

But Reggae kept running. Then she stopped and sat, her tail wagging furiously. It was as if she thought she'd done something extremely clever.

Josh ran towards her. Then he saw the fox cub. He was nuzzling his mother who was lying on the ground. She'd been shot. Probably earlier in the day.

'Good pup,' Josh said to Reggae.

Without picking her up, he checked the cub's eyes. They were open. That was good. It meant he was more than a couple of weeks old, and had a chance of surviving without her mother.

Then he picked him up carefully by the scruff of the neck (he'd been bitten twice before by cubs). He examined his mouth (yes, sharp teeth) and her leg muscles (she could get around).

'About six weeks old,' he told Reggae. 'So she's not for us. We'll take her to Joanne.' The butcher's wife would be delighted.

He put the cub down and started to search the ground for the den. If there was one cub still alive, there were probably others nearby. And Joanne always said the more, the merrier.

*   *   *

'Go,' Josh said. Reggae ran the few steps to her food bowl, and started to eat.

'You're doing well,' Josh told her. 'But you still have a long way to go. So do I.'

Josh knew that he'd have to get permission from the vet to take part in the Gathering. And because the Gathering, and the gruelling fank afterwards, was such a severe test for a dog, it would be no easy thing to get the vet to agree to let a dog as young as Reggae participate. Josh was pretty sure *he* could do the ten days of hard physical labour involved . . . but Reggae? She might *think* she was a lion, but she was just over a year old. And she still spent most of her time in the shed, sleeping.

It wasn't just her fitness. There was still so much for Reggae to learn. She'd never practised driving sheep or splitting them. Even dogs with years of experience had trouble splitting sheep.

Josh looked up. Reggae was peering at him, with her head tilted. It looked like she'd been there for a while.

Josh rubbed her head.

'It's no big deal. I'm just a bit tongue-tied with the vet. I've never managed to say anything very much to him.'

The second time Josh had met the vet was when his uncle had called him to deal with a crack in their bull's front hoof. Josh knew Calum was upset because of the expense, but *he'd* been really pleased to think he was going to see the vet again. He wanted to tell him about all the animals he'd rescued.

The scene came vividly back to Josh. He'd met the brightly coloured van in the yard.

'Hi Josh,' the vet said. 'Up to any mischief?'

Josh had intended to tell him there and then about the animals he'd rescued from round the croft. But nothing would come out of his mouth. He just felt like a stupid little boy who wanted to speak to a king.

The vet must have realised he wanted to talk – so he waited – what seemed like forever. Then he shrugged, picked up his bag and went to tend the bull, saying over his shoulder, 'I'll be glad to hear what it is you're wanting to tell me, when you're ready.'

Josh followed him like an orphaned puppy to the crush, where the bull would be held still so the vet could work on him, and then back to the van when he'd finished, all the time trying to make some words come out of his mouth.

In the end he'd not been able to say a single thing. Except 'bye'. He would have to say a lot more than that to persuade the vet to let Reggae take part in the Gathering.

Reggae was looking at Josh, keen to move on. She trusted him to make everything all right.

'Don't worry. I'm on top of this. I'll talk him into it. Somehow.'

Chapter 13

Josh decided it would be easiest for him (and Yvonne) if they didn't bump into one another for a couple of days. She was better off with Eric really.

By ducking into the classes they shared late and dashing off at the end, he'd avoided her the first half of the day. At the end of English, he'd seen her getting up to follow him, but he'd given her the slip in the crowded hallway.

Now there was just lunch and one more class to go. He headed for the library and was completely absorbed in watching a video showing a dog trainer teaching 'driving' when he felt a tap on his shoulder.

He looked up. Yvonne. Her face was flushed and her lips tight.

'What's going on?' she demanded.

'Going on?'

'You know what I mean. You've been avoiding me all day. And yesterday.'

'Quiet!' the librarian shouted. Yvonne flushed even deeper. But she didn't take her angry eyes off Josh. Everyone in the library was staring at them.

Josh's brain felt as if it had short-circuited. Why was Yvonne making a fuss? He was giving her 'space', wasn't he? He couldn't compete with the likes of Eric.

Yvonne's face got darker. Somehow she managed

to whisper even louder than she had spoken earlier. 'I asked, what is going on?'

Josh blurted out, 'But you like Eric!'

For a moment, Yvonne looked bewildered. Then in quick succession, a light came into her eyes, she looked up at the ceiling and sat heavily on the chair next to Josh.

'Is that what this is all about?'

'I didn't want to get in the way,' Josh explained.

'Get in the way of what?'

'You and Eric.'

'Me and Eric what?'

'You like him . . .'

Yvonne rolled her eyes. 'We're doing a maths project together.'

'He's smart, like you.'

Yvonne giggled. The librarian gave her another look. 'You're getting me in a lot of trouble,' she whispered, as she tried to get control of herself.

'I don't mean to.'

'Do you really think I'd disappear the day after I met your lovely dog?'

'People *do* just disappear . . .' Josh blurted out. And suddenly his eyes started to water. Desperately, he fought back the unexpected emotion.

'Oh,' Yvonne said.

His hand felt the whisper of her touch. He turned away towards the computer monitor. *Why* did all these feelings about his mother keep coming up? On the screen, he watched the trainer kneeling, rubbing his dog's tummy. Somehow this calmed him.

Yvonne continued to sit next to him, watching him intently.

The bell rang.

'Are you okay?' Yvonne asked.

'He's really good,' Josh said, pointing at the trainer in the video.

Yvonne sighed, nodding. Then she persisted. 'Are *we* okay?'

Josh nodded but he didn't meet her eye. He didn't trust himself to speak.

'Do you want to walk to music class?' Yvonne picked up her bag.

Josh closed the browser and stood.

*   *   *

A few days later, Josh powered up the steep valley slope, with Reggae bounding along by his side. Just above the secret valley, he stopped to survey the surrounding area. There was no one in sight.

Josh knelt down so that he was on Reggae's level. He could feel the warm sun on his face. 'Today, you're going to learn how to drive sheep,' he told her. 'That's when you work on the same side of the sheep as me. In the Gathering, once we've collected the sheep, we get behind them and drive them to the pens where they're tagged and treated.'

Josh led Reggae down the slope, until they were relatively close to a group of sheep. He stopped. Reggae's body tensed as she awaited the command to go off to her right.

'Heel,' Josh said. He took a step forward. Reggae stayed where she was, looking off to their right. Josh turned and gave her a stern look, pointing to his side. Reluctantly, Reggae took a step forward.

Josh took another stop. Reggae hesitated again. She was still expecting to do an outrun.

Then, with a terrible shock, Josh became aware of somebody coming over the hill! Somebody with two dogs. He'd been concentrating so much on Reggae, he'd forgotten to keep an eye out.

'Down!' he whispered urgently and he followed his own command, plunging to the ground. Had they seen him? *Had they seen Reggae?*

He had to get them both out of sight! He lifted his head and looked around. There were a couple of tall gorse bushes not too far away. They could hide behind them.

'Come,' he whispered, and he started to crawl along the ground on his stomach. Reggae wagged her tail and crept along by his side. To her, this was a wonderful new game.

Safely hidden behind the bush, Josh tried to compose himself. Who was this person? And why was he in *his* valley?

Chapter 14

Josh felt like a mouse trapped by a cat. But who was the cat? Kneeling, he peered through the yellow gorse flowers.

From this distance, all he could see was a dark, hooded man with heavy eyebrows. He was shouting angrily at his two dogs, who were running around wildly and barking. The man wasn't looking in his direction. Josh breathed a sigh of relief. They hadn't been spotted.

As the man came down the hill, Josh got a clearer look. His heart sank. It was Dunham, a man who was hated and feared, both for his fierce and uncontrolled temper and his shady practices. Josh had heard many stories about Dunham told by his uncle's friends over late-night drinks. How he'd been caught stealing wood from someone's forest – and almost beat to death the man who found him at it. And how he always remembered a grievance, seeking revenge even years later.

Josh had no trouble believing these stories, because Kearney was Dunham's son. A bully cut from the same mould as his father.

Why had Dunham sought out such a hidden valley? A place far away from where he lived?

Josh watched as Dunham placed himself in front

of a small group of ewes. Josh tickled Reggae behind her right ear. Fortunately, he didn't have to worry about *her* making any noise.

Dunham's dogs were running back and forth on long leads, barking excitedly. They hardly paid any attention to their master's commands.

He shouted their names, again and again. Eventually when they came to heel Dunham struck each dog hard on the head. Josh inhaled sharply. What was the point of that? It would just teach them not to come when he called the next time.

Josh took several deep breaths, trying to calm himself. He hated to see animals badly treated. Especially Border collies. And it wasn't just the dogs . . . What would these bullied and badly-trained dogs do to the commons sheep, *his* sheep, the ones he'd been using to train Reggae?

'Away,' Dunham ordered. The two dogs headed straight for the sheep, barking loudly. Alarmed, the ewes scattered. It was then Josh saw the green markings on the right thigh of several of the sheep. They belonged to his uncle! They must have escaped onto the commons through the broken fence Calum had been muttering about mending for weeks. Using the long leads, Dunham hauled the dogs back. Then he hit them again. 'To the right, you stupid mutts.'

Dunham ordered the dogs off again. This time, at least they went to their right. But rather than finding the balancing point, one dog charged one of his uncle's ewes and bit her behind the ear. The other dog jumped on the back of a young lamb, also with his uncle's mark, who bleated in shock and pain. When its mother rounded on him, both dogs attacked her, tearing off mouthfuls of fleece. The ewe and her lamb cried out in pain.

Dunham watched the attack in silence. Then he called the dogs. Eventually, ears low and heads down, they returned. He patted them on their side.

'That's right,' he said. 'Show 'em who's boss.'

Josh couldn't believe what he'd seen. How could Dunham think it was all right to treat sheep that way? Didn't he realise those animals were his uncle's? In fact it didn't matter who they belonged to. It was a serious crime to mistreat sheep.

Josh sat down heavily behind the gorse. His uncle's ewe had been attacked for defending her own lamb. He couldn't let this go on. But then he remembered what Dunham had done to the crofter who found him stealing wood . . . Josh shivered, in spite of the warmth of the day. If he interfered, he – and Reggae – could be in serious danger.

Josh wished suddenly he could just call his uncle on a mobile. But the mobile phone he'd been promised the previous Christmas had never appeared. It probably wouldn't have worked out here anyway, he consoled himself. The reception would be terrible so far from a mast. There was nobody he could call for help. It was up to him.

The sound of frantic barking interrupted his thoughts. Dunham's dogs were now chasing a young lamb up the hill. Josh spotted the green marking. Suddenly the lamb disappeared.

She'd been so frantic she hadn't looked where she was going! She must have fallen into a hole. Dunham called the dogs and sent them on another outrun. He didn't even bother to check if the lamb was all right.

Over the years, Josh had found several sheep who had broken their legs in such holes. What kind of an animal rescuer was he if he allowed this to go on?

He began to examine the area behind the gorse bush. *If* he was going to interfere, he didn't want Dunham to think he'd been sitting here, watching him. He had to appear from somewhere else, as if he'd just come upon the scene. That would be the best way of protecting Reggae, and himself.

Josh could see a slight depression in the ground, not too far behind the gorse bush. It seemed to run along the ground up the side of the hill. If he could get to the depression, maybe he could crawl along and appear from someplace else?

Reggae made a soft noise in her throat. She was standing right in front of him, gazing at him with her head tilted. He knew that look. She was concerned about him. She licked his shirt. It was soaked! He hadn't realised that he was sweating.

Then Josh understood. He was thinking of going up against the most feared man on the island. No wonder he was sweating!

'I'm okay,' Josh whispered, rubbing between Reggae's eyes.

But Josh knew he *wasn't* okay. He was about to take the biggest risk of his life. And Reggae somehow knew it.

She licked his face, her head still tilted.

'All right,' Josh said softly. 'I *am* a bit frightened. Wish me luck.'

Josh took another glance through the gorse bush. Dunham and his dogs were on the other side of the valley now, facing the opposite way. This was his chance.

'Down. Stay.' Then he got down on his belly, and crawled towards the lower ground.

Chapter 15

Josh couldn't crawl any further. The lower ground that kept him hidden from Dunham ended just a few yards ahead. He turned his head to try to work out the distance he'd come. Was it far enough away from the bush where Reggae was hiding?

He didn't know. But he did know that if he continued to crawl, he'd be visible, and *that* would be a disaster. Would the story he'd worked out – that he was going to his Aunt Gertrude's house – convince Dunham? It was true she spent a lot of time on the mainland, but he was pretty sure she was on the island now. Would Dunham know better? He was aware of a tremor in his legs. Did he really want to do this? As if to answer his question, a chorus of squeals and cries came from the sheep in the valley. Dunham's dogs were at it again.

One . . . two . . . two and a half . . . Josh gathered himself and stood up. He started walking, as casually as he could, on an angle across the valley and away from Dunham. If his plan didn't work . . . he didn't want to think about that.

The next time he heard the dogs barking, he turned toward Dunham.

'Hello, Mr Redlin,' he shouted, as cheerily as he could manage. His voice cracked as he said

Dunham's name. Don't show how scared you are, he told himself.

Surprise, anger, guilt and fear flitted over the man's face in quick succession.

'Getting your dogs up to speed for the Gathering?' Josh called, as if he'd just arrived on the scene. He walked towards Dunham and his dogs, in what he hoped was a neighbourly way.

Dunham moved swiftly to intercept him, trying to prevent Josh from getting too close to the sheep. As Josh had planned, this took him – and his dogs – further away from where Reggae was hidden. Josh stopped and waited. His knees felt like they'd turned to Play Doh.

'Lovely day for it,' Josh said, when Dunham got close enough to talk in a conversational tone.

'Yes,' Dunham's answer was curt. 'What are you doing here?' He wasn't bothering to hide his hostility.

'I'm on my way to my aunt's.'

Dunham clearly didn't believe him. He glanced at Josh's trousers. Josh looked down at them. They were coated with dirt from crawling along the ground! He was horrified. 'I tripped and slid down a slope,' he improvised.

'Front first?' Dunham asked sceptically.

At first, Josh didn't understand what he was getting at. Then he realised all the dirt was on the *front* side of his trousers. Because he'd been crawling.

Dunham's dogs were growling, as if reflecting their master's aggression. Josh had to change the subject. He knelt down and showed them the

back of his hand. 'Lovely dogs,' he said, warmly.

One of the two dogs inched closer. Josh tickled him behind his ear.

'No need for that,' Dunham said.

Josh suddenly noticed the dog's distinctive markings, a white patch around his left eye. 'Is this Kearney's dog?'

'*Kearney*'s dog?' Dunham said dismissively. 'I wouldn't let that lad *near* any of my working animals. He's hopeless.' He looked on, irritated, as his second dog came to Josh, wanting some affection. Josh stroked the side of his head.

Josh couldn't help feeling pleased he'd discovered Kearney had made up the story about 'his' dog. But now he had to come up with a lie himself. One that would fool Dunham. He continued to stroke the dogs – touching an animal helped him think. Then he had it. 'The thing is,' he said to Dunham, as if confessing a crime. 'I like to rescue small animals that are hurt. I must have got my trousers dirty when I was crawling towards the fox den I discovered yesterday.'

'You like to rescue animals?' Dunham said, with a crooked smile. He clearly thought Josh was an idiot. He pulled on the leads, forcing the dogs towards him.

Josh stood. He couldn't leave yet. If he did Dunham would just go back to working his dogs. And hurting the sheep. 'I'd better get going,' Josh said.

Dunham relaxed and moved to shake his hand. But as he did so, Josh looked beyond him and pointed. 'Oh, no, look!' he said, in what he hoped was a surprised tone of voice. 'That ewe belongs to my uncle.'

Dunham interrupted in a low, threatening voice. 'You'll not be accusing me of hurting another man's sheep?'

So he *had* recognised Uncle Calum's green brand! Josh didn't respond directly. 'They must have escaped through a hole in our fence.' he said.

'You didn't answer my question.'

Josh was glad his loose trousers hid his shaking knees. He had to stand firm.

'*Have* they been hurt?' he asked, as if he didn't know already.

'If they have, it wasn't by me.'

'Then why would I accuse you of anything?' Josh replied.

Dunham glowered. But Josh's logic was hard to argue with. 'Right,' he said. 'I'm done for the day. You'd better get those sheep back to your uncle.' He started to drag his dogs away. They looked longingly at Josh. He guessed they didn't get much affection. Josh hesitated. Then he started to walk towards the ewe who was 'mawing' for her lamb.

Dunham wasn't expecting that. 'Where are you going?' he demanded.

'That ewe over there is distressed,' Josh pointed.

Dunham's face went dark, like clouds before a storm. Josh could see his struggle to control himself. The dark-eyed man knew what Josh would find.

'Why don't I come with you to check it out?' he said, tightening the lead on his dogs.

They walked together awkwardly. As they got nearer to the hole in which the lamb had fallen, the dogs started to bark with excitement.

Dunham pulled sharply on their leads. 'Shut up.'

'That's why she's calling,' Josh said, trying to keep his voice even. 'Her lamb's in the hole there.'

'What a shame,' Dunham said.

'It mustn't have been looking where it was going,' Josh said carefully.

'That's right.'

Josh jumped down into the hole, and helped the frightened lamb to her feet. He felt up and down each leg carefully. Nothing seemed to be broken. Then he noticed the bite wounds near the lamb's tail. He inspected the wound with his hand. He felt two sticky spots. The dog had drawn blood.

If he said anything about the wound, Dunham would deny any knowledge of it. And he couldn't say he'd seen the dog jump on the lamb's back because Dunham would know he'd been watching from behind the gorse bush. So Josh said nothing. He picked up the lamb and lifted her above his head, placing her on the higher ground. Dunham didn't do anything to help. He had his hands full restraining his dogs. The ewe ran towards the lamb and immediately started licking it clean.

Josh pulled himself out of the hole.

Dunham looked relieved. 'Happens to my lambs all the time. They haven't got a brain in their heads. No harm done then,' he said warningly.

Josh hesitated, then, thinking of Reggae, he nodded. 'No harm done.'

Dunham stared at the dirt on Josh's trousers, still suspicious. 'I don't like being played for a fool.'

Josh held up his empty hands, in a gesture of peace. 'There's nothing to worry about, Mr Redlin. I'll call my uncle from my aunt's house. He'll come and get his sheep.'

'You won't say anything about me and my dogs . . .'

Josh shrugged. 'What's to say? You have a right to work them.'

'That's right. I have a right,' Dunham agreed.

'Sorry to disturb you. I'll be off then,' Josh said politely, heading off in the direction of his aunt's.

Dunham dragged his dogs off in the opposite direction.

Josh carried on until he was sure that Dunham was well out of sight. He just hoped that Reggae had stayed where she was.

Then he turned and, following a circuitous route, returned to the valley. This gave him plenty of time to think. And none of what he thought made him feel any better.

Dunham hadn't believed Josh's story about the fox's den. And he wouldn't like the fact that Josh now suspected Dunham's dogs had hurt his uncle's sheep. He would want to find some way to make sure Josh kept his mouth shut.

When he reached the gorse bush Reggae was on her feet, breathing rapidly. She charged over to him and jumped up on his chest.

'Good girl. It's all over,' Josh said, patting her reassuringly. 'You're safe. That was really bad luck. He'll be keeping an eye on our valley from now on. We can't train here any more. But he won't be back today.' He scanned the valley just to be sure. 'At least we can round up Calum's sheep, show them how well-trained dogs behave.'

Reggae sat, quivering with excitement. At last she was going to work!

Chapter 16

The following day, Josh walked to school with legs that were heavy and lifeless. Sleep had seemed within reach all night, only to retreat when he got near. He kept remembering Dunham's words, 'I don't like being played for a fool.' What might that mean?

Josh had spent part of the night trying to think of another secluded part of the commons where he and Reggae could work without having to worry about being discovered. The only place he could think of would take ages to get to. Reggae's training time would be greatly reduced. And all this just at the time he really had to ramp up the preparation.

It was about three in the morning that he'd started to question himself. What had ever made him think that *he* could train a dog? *In less than a year?* The very idea was ridiculous. He'd totally messed it up. He'd started way too late. He'd done two long outruns with her, but the Gathering required tons of long outruns, all at a much greater distance than they'd ever attempted. The most gruelling test of man and dog . . . and he thought he could get a dog in shape for *that*?

As he trudged through the stand of trees, his eyes firmly focused on the ground, Josh felt a tap on his shoulder.

'Are you still ignoring me?'

Yvonne.

'No,' he said in a flat voice. 'I'm just tired. I didn't sleep last night.' Quickly, he filled her in on what had happened. 'I should have kept my mouth shut.'

'You couldn't let that man's dogs hurt your uncle's sheep!'

'Reggae's my priority.'

'You wouldn't be you if you let someone hurt animals – your uncle's, or anyone else's,' Yvonne declared firmly.

Josh felt comforted by this. Even if he wasn't sure Yvonne was right.

But she had more to say. 'I've got news. About the Gathering!'

'Yes?'

'I heard my dad on the phone,' Yvonne told him. 'He's found a new parasite on the commons' sheep. He's decided to move the Gathering forward two weeks so they can treat it before it affects the health of the rest of the sheep on the island.'

'They can't do that!' Josh protested. But before he could say another word, somebody barged between them.

'What's the Gathering to you?' Kearney demanded. 'You're not thinking of working in the pens are you, City Boy?'

'So what if I was?'

Kearney laughed loudly. 'The island men would eat you for lunch.'

'Kearney,' Yvonne protested.

Josh could have sworn that for a millisecond Kearney looked hurt. But even if he was, his words were full of scorn.

'You're not really encouraging this loser to work in the Gathering?' He barged Josh again.

Josh had had enough. He didn't want Yvonne to think he couldn't defend himself.

'Talking about losers,' he said. 'How's your dog?'

For a moment, Kearney looked thrown.

Josh went on. 'Remember? You told me about him in the library – the one with a white patch around his left eye.' Josh savoured the moment. For once, he wasn't being bullied by Kearney. *He* had the power. Kearney seemed to shrink. 'I saw him yesterday, "your" Border. Your father laughed when I asked him if she was yours . . . He said he'd never let you near any of his dogs.'

Kearney stared at him. Just for a second Josh imagined red rays coming out of the boy's eyes and converging on his heart – stopping it dead. Then Kearney shot a quick glance at Yvonne. His shoulders slumped.

'You feel pretty clever now, don't you?' he snarled. 'It won't last. I'll make sure of that.'

With that, Kearney stalked off ahead of them.

'Josh!' Yvonne said, frowning.

'He deserved it,' Josh asserted.

'Get off,' Yvonne said sharply. 'Would you kick a dog?'

'That's different!'

They walked together in silence. Josh's face was

burning. In successive days, he'd managed to make enemies of the two biggest bullies on the island, father and son.

'I shouldn't have done that.' He admitted after a bit. 'I hope he's wrong about the island men.'

'Of course he is,' Yvonne said. 'They'll judge you by what you can do.'

'With two weeks less to train Reggae now, that may not be much.'

Yvonne stopped and turned to him. 'Be realistic, Josh. No one trains a dog in the time you've got. You just have to make sure she can do the basics. And when are you going to talk to my dad? You still need to get his permission to take part.'

'He's not "your dad" to me,' Josh said quietly as they set off once again.

'He isn't an ogre.'

'It's not that!' Josh said, anguished. 'I've *never* been able to talk to him.'

They could see the school yard ahead. Josh felt exhausted, both from lack of sleep and the events of the previous day.

As they arrived at the school gate, Yvonne slapped her head. 'I almost forgot! I've got something for you.'

She took off her school rucksack and shoved her hand deep into one of its pockets. She removed a small plastic object. 'It's an old MP3 player. Now that I've got a new phone, I don't use it anymore.'

Josh felt confused. Surely Yvonne knew that listening to music wasn't high on his list of things to do in the coming days. But he didn't want to seem ungrateful. 'Thank you,' he said, not really meaning it.

'Is that the best you can do?'

'I don't have time to listen to music,' Josh said, defensively.

'I know that,' Yvonne exclaimed. 'Have a little faith.' She assumed a dramatic pose. 'Ta da! There's an audio recording of "A Midsummer Night's Dream" on it. The Shakespeare play we're studying in class?'

'Really?' Josh asked. 'You mean I don't have to read it?'

'It's not a replacement for reading,' Yvonne said primly. 'It's an aid. Which you can listen to before our tutorial.'

'You're brilliant!' Josh exclaimed.

Yvonne's face glowed. 'That's more like it,' she said quietly.

Chapter 17

Josh and Calum carried the roll of fencing between them. The dew in the pasture glistened in the early morning sun. His uncle liked to start errands early on a Saturday, which suited Josh, as it meant he was free in the afternoon.

Fortunately, it wasn't a full roll. Those weighed a ton.

They walked in silence, dressed in their work clothes: loose jeans and flannel shirts. Calum wore a worn grey rucksack, full of tools, U nails, a staple gun and other items they might need.

'Josh, I'll be out Thursday night at the Crofters' Association meeting,' said Calum. 'And Saturday a couple of my old friends from the SFU – the Farmers' Union – will be coming over for a drink and some dinner.'

'No problem,' Josh said. That meant he could spend more time with Reggae on Thursday, and maybe see Yvonne on the Saturday.

They walked on in silence. Then Calum began again.

'I was thinking about the other day. When you found our sheep on the commons. How did you manage to gather two lambs and two ewes and bring them back on your own?'

Josh stumbled. He'd deliberately been vague about the number of sheep that he'd found. How had Calum figured it out?

Then Josh knew – by the state of their fleece and the wounds that Dunham's dogs had inflicted. Calum must've inspected the whole flock. As Calum well knew, it was almost impossible to gather four sheep on your own. Even two was a stretch without a dog.

'Normally, it would have been hopeless,' Josh said. 'But just by chance I had a couple of long ropes in my rucksack.'

Josh was happy to leave it at that. But Calum wasn't.

'I still don't get how you managed to get them *together*.'

Josh's mind spun like a hamster on a wheel, rejecting one possible explanation after another.

'They weren't that far away. You know the gorge with the wooden fence around it, on the way to Alastair's house?'

After a moment Calum replied, 'Yes. Watch this hole here.'

They manoeuvred the roll of wire around the erosion hole.

'Well, they were grazing against the fence. I had some Polo mints in my pocket. From lunch. I some-times give them to the sheep as a treat.'

'You lured them using mints?' Calum didn't sound at all convinced.

'The two ewes had tasted them before. They knew it was a treat. I got hold of the lambs when they came to get milk. It took a while.'

'I'll bet it did!' Calum exclaimed.

'It was one of those times a mobile would have been handy,' Josh said quietly. 'Or a dog.'

Calum ignored the comment about the phone. 'A working dog *would* be handy . . . This way.'

Josh wondered what Calum meant. Did he suspect something?

They reached the fence and got to work. Josh stood by one post holding the tape measure as Calum walked to the next one. They needed to replace the whole length.

A few months ago on his way home from school, Josh had seen one of the islanders repair a fence by weaving new fencing into the broken strands. He'd asked Calum about this.

'He thinks he doesn't have time to do a proper job,' Calum had said. 'But he'll have to repair it again within the year. And if he didn't have time to do it right the first time, when will he have time to do it over?'

At first, Josh had thought Calum was nit-picking, but later he'd seen the same crofter repairing the fence again. And he'd realised Calum was right. It was better to do things properly the first time.

'Four metres,' Calum announced. He pulled out

two pairs of worn leather gloves from his rucksack, and threw a pair to Josh.

They unrolled the fencing and measured out four and a half metres. Calum stapled the old wire to the first post. Then, while Josh held the new wire in place, Calum stapled it too.

This was the easy part. What was hard was stretching the wire tight to the next post, and holding it while it too was fastened securely. This was Josh's job. He remembered the first time he'd done it, several years earlier. He'd still had city muscles, then. They'd had to come back a couple of months later to tighten what he'd done.

Josh anchored his feet to the ground, and started to pull the wire tight. His arms ached.

Calum got the staple gun ready. 'So you noticed the sheep had been attacked?' he asked.

Josh almost lost his grip but recovered quickly. 'Of course.'

'And you have no idea how it happened.'

'No,' Josh said, trying to sound convincing. 'It must have happened before I found them.'

Calum started stapling. When he finished, Josh relaxed his grip. He stretched out his arms and made several fists with his hands to release the tension.

'I can't think what would have done that kind of damage,' Calum said. 'Except a badly trained dog.'

Had Calum guessed? Josh hoped not. But what if *Dunham* found out about Reggae? He might tell everyone it was *Josh*'s dog that had hurt the sheep!

115

'A *really* badly trained dog,' Josh agreed carefully. 'Either a wild dog, or one whose owner didn't care about other people's sheep.'

Calum nodded slowly. 'I don't like to think there's anyone like that on the island.'

Josh said nothing. He knew only too well there was.

Chapter 18

'The idea is not to *guess* the name of the angle,' Yvonne said, in a frustrated tone. She was beginning to lose patience. Josh didn't blame her. His second maths tutorial was turning out exactly as he'd feared – Yvonne was beginning to see what a total dummy he was.

'I'm trying!' he protested. 'No one talks about "acute" or "obtuse" angles in real life.'

'Just memorise it!' Yvonne said. 'Acute is less than 90 degrees, obtuse more.'

'It's all right for you,' Josh snapped. 'Your brain absorbs everything you put into it. Mine's different. Things have to make sense to me.'

Yvonne just stared at him. Then she nodded, as if to herself.

Josh watched his friend. Was it all over? Had she decided she had better ways to spend her time?

'Okay,' she said calmly. 'Then we need to find a way to have it make sense . . .' She stared into space for a moment. 'I've got it!'

She grabbed a blank sheet of paper and drew a group of animals on it – Josh could tell they had four legs, but he wasn't sure what they were supposed to be.

'Dogs?' he guessed.

'Sheep,' Yvonne corrected, with a small smile. 'A group of sheep.' She drew a line behind them. 'And this is a cliff.'

'Okay.'

Under the sheep, Yvonne put a large X and a small x next to each other. 'These are you and Reggae.'

Josh nodded.

'If you say to Reggae, "away", where will she go?'

On the piece of paper, Josh showed her where Reggae would run – anti-clockwise around the sheep.

Yvonne jabbed her finger onto the paper at a point on the dog's journey. 'What kind of an angle do you have here? Less than 90 degrees or more?'

Suddenly, Josh understood where Yvonne was going. 'More. And if I said "come by", she'd go clockwise. And then, the angle would be less than 90 degrees!'

'Just remember this picture,' Yvonne said. '*Away* means "obtuse", *come by* means "acute".'

Josh felt a huge smile spread across his face. 'Have I ever told you you're brilliant?' he said.

Yvonne looked away and smiled shyly. 'Twice in one week . . . not that I'm counting . . .'

* * *

Josh whistled as he walked along the road. It was a tune that had come back to him the night before – 'Jamming'. His mum used to sing it to him. He only vaguely remembered the chorus. But his mum had explained that it meant the two of them would

118

always win out in spite of everything. He'd certainly felt good when she was singing to him . . .

He turned into the car park of the small general store. As was his custom, he quickly walked along the five small aisles, to make sure no one he knew was there. Then he picked up a small plastic basket and pulled out the shopping list his uncle had written in his crabbed handwriting. A tin of kidney beans, Bisto and apples. First he picked up a couple of tins of dog food for Reggae then, smiling as he remembered Yvonne's drawing of sheep, he grabbed a bag of apples and went in search of the gravy mix.

'This isn't your local store.' A gruff voice interrupted his train of thought. Startled, he looked up to find Dunham peering down at him. 'Been to your aunt's again? The one on the mainland?' he asked sarcastically.

Josh froze. There was *dog food* in the basket! Quickly, he shifted it to his left hand, so that it was half-hidden between him and the shelves of food. As if to explain this movement he extended his right hand to Dunham.

But Dunham ignored it. 'You haven't told anybody about meeting me the other day?'

'No!' Josh said, in a high-pitched voice. He struggled to control his shock and fear. 'I said I wouldn't.' That sounded better.

Dunham smiled, as if he found something very amusing. 'It's our little secret, is it?'

Josh nodded, not understanding what was so funny.

Dunham turned away with a twisted smile that somehow scared Josh more than the threats he'd made the other day. 'Our little secret,' he repeated under his breath, as if such a good joke had to be savoured.

*　*　*

Josh was furious with himself. How could he have been so absent-minded? He couldn't afford to relax, especially now that the Gathering was so close.

Had Dunham seen the dog food? Josh pictured the basket in his head. The tins had been pretty well hidden by the bag of apples. And he'd put it all out of sight almost immediately. Surely Dunham would have made a comment if he'd seen it. And even if he had, he'd think Josh was buying it for someone else. Josh breathed a sigh of relief. He'd got away with it. This time.

Josh knew Dunham didn't like trusting him not to say anything. Dunham didn't trust anyone. But surely he must realise that Josh *hadn't* said anything about the attack on the sheep – Calum would have been knocking on his door if he had. Which meant Dunham *could* trust Josh.

*　*　*

As he neared Reggae's shed, Josh looked cautiously around, to make sure no one saw him go up to it. Like closing the stable door after the horse has bolted, he thought bitterly. Still, he couldn't let the lapse in his attention become a habit.

'I'm here,' he whispered. He heard Reggae panting inside.

He opened the door and the little dog was upon him, licking his face. Josh had taken her for a long run before he'd gone to Yvonne's for his tutorial. But he knew Reggae would have preferred to spend more time with him. At least she hadn't been tied up outside the shop when Dunham had appeared . . .

He opened the tin of dog food and put it into Reggae's dish. She sat obediently, waiting for Josh to release her, salivating at the thought of dinner.

'Give me five,' Josh said. Reggae held out her right paw. Josh shook it. 'Now the other five.' Reggae held out her left paw. 'Good girl. Go.'

Reggae charged over to the bowl and started eating noisily.

Josh told her about his day, and about his second tutorial with Yvonne. 'If anyone can teach me, she can.'

He decided Reggae didn't need to know about his encounter with Dunham. It would just worry her.

He just wished he knew what Dunham had found so amusing.

Chapter 19

Josh wasn't sure how he was going to get to sleep. He'd been lying in the dark for hours already. His room was like a steam bath. And his mind kept going back to his encounter with Dunham . . . and his 'joke'.

Thinking about Dunham reminded him of Kearney. Yvonne hadn't brought it up again, but he knew she was unhappy with what Josh had done. And if he was honest with himself, it didn't sit well with him either. It had left a sour taste in his mouth. He didn't like to think of himself as a bully. He wasn't! But that meant he owed Kearney an apology.

He checked the Velux window again. It was open as far as it could go. But without any other window there was no chance of a through draft of cooler air, and so the room, just under the roof still hot from the day's sun, just would not cool down.

He glanced at the digital clock. Midnight. How *was* he going to go to sleep? He took out Yvonne's MP3 player. Maybe "A Midsummer Night's Dream" would do the trick. He was in the middle of Act 2. This was his third go through the whole thing. He was finding that even the speeches that at first had seemed like a foreign language to him were now making sense.

Josh fumbled with the player in the dark. The sound of a rap artist came through the headphones. For a moment he was confused. Then he realised it was a radio station. He fiddled with the dial, rapidly passing through traditional music, pop music, French conversation. Then he found something which was familiar. Reggae. Josh settled into the pillow and started to relax. His mother used to play music like this to him at night. Marley, Toots and the Maytals, Jimmy Cliff. He'd always thought she did this to put him to sleep. Though as he listened now, he realised these songs were about as far away from lullabies as you could get, with their heavy beat and rousing words.

Suddenly, he realised his mum *hadn't* played reggae at night to put him to sleep. She'd played it because *she* liked it. There was something she'd called herself . . . what was it? A white rasta! That was it!

He still found it hard to imagine his white rasta mother and Calum were brother and sister. Calum did like fiery music like his mum . . . but for Calum, it was traditional fiddlers playing at a hectic pace.

But strangely, listening to the reggae *did* make him feel tired. He closed his eyes and a memory popped into his head: how his mother would sit by his bed, talking to him, and the way, when the music moved her, she'd stand to dance, even in the middle of a conversation or story. He could almost see her small body swaying and bobbing alongside his bed, as sleep claimed him.

* * *

'In the morning,' Josh explained to Yvonne as they walked to school, 'I found my headphones on the pillow. Actually your headphones. They were playing something completely different. I hope the reggae wasn't a one-off.'

They were approaching the school now. People were being dropped off from cars, and walking towards the gate from every direction. A sea of green uniforms.

'It may be a regular show. You can look up the station's schedule on the web. But you still have to listen to "A Midsummer Night's Dream".'

'That's no problem,' Josh replied. 'I like listening to it. Still, if they played reggae every night, I'd never have trouble falling asleep. It makes me feel my mother is still close.'

As they went through the gate, Josh saw a group of boys clustered around Kearney at the other side of the yard. It looked like they were passing an object from hand to hand. When a boy got the object, he'd put it up to his eyes and swivel around to face a group of girls standing just outside the entrance to the school. Then he would hand it to another boy.

Josh was reminded of his resolution the night before. He had to apologise. . . . But surely he should wait until it was *just* Kearney . . . No, Josh told himself. You're making excuses. Now or never.

'I've got to talk to Kearney,' he said to Yvonne. They walked towards the group. As they got closer, Josh saw the object being handed to Kearney, who swivelled and faced him and Yvonne.

Binoculars. Kearney was watching him through

them. Josh felt like a bug under a microscope, but he'd promised himself he'd do the right thing.

The walk across the playground took forever. Kearney must've been given the binoculars as a present, and brought them to school to show them off.

When he was just a couple of feet away, Kearney took them down from his eyes. Everyone was staring at Josh now.

'I wanted to apologise for what I said the other day,' he said.

For the briefest of moments, Josh thought Kearney was taken aback, vulnerable even. Then his face reset into its normal sneer.

'You? Apologise to me? What could you ever possibly do that would hurt me?' Kearney laughed at the thought, and his gang, taking their lead from him, joined in.

Josh stood there, paralysed. Yvonne gently put her hand on his back and steered him away.

Angus said loudly. 'He needs a *girl* to rescue him!'

The boys laughed and made catcalls. Josh wished he could disappear into a hole in the ground. If this was what happened when you did the right thing . . .

Strangely though, Kearney didn't join in with his friends – he *wasn't* laughing, or shouting at Josh. He just watched as Yvonne led him away.

* * *

'There's a lot of talk about immigration in the papers at the moment,' Mr Sampson began their history class. 'Where did the people on this island come from?'

'My family's always been here,' a blond boy asserted. 'For hundreds of years.'

'Mine too,' several other dark-haired children chimed in.

'In fact,' Mr Sampson said, 'Everyone on this island has come from somewhere else. There have been at least five distinct waves of immigration, including the Vikings. Today, I'd like to think about immigration and how it has shaped who we are.'

Josh could hardly believe his ears. *Everyone* on the island had come from somewhere else? Then the only difference between himself and the people who saw him as a 'blow-in' was that they 'blew in' a few years earlier!

He thought, 'Thank you, Mr Sampson.'

* * *

As Josh headed home, his heart lifted as it always did, when he was about to see Reggae. He was walking alone this afternoon. Yvonne was at maths club. This meant he could go at his normal speed. Yvonne always struggled to keep up with him.

Thinking about Yvonne reminded him of her MP3 player. He stopped, pulled it out of his rucksack, and put on the white headphones. He switched from the radio station he'd been listening to the previous night to 'A Midsummer Night's Dream'. It was one of his favourite bits, in which Titania the fairy queen falls in love with the character called Bottom.

As Josh emerged from the woods, he looked around to make sure he was alone. Then he headed up the hill to the boundaries of his uncle's farm. On the player, the theatrical troupe were starting to rehearse their play. As usual, Bottom was being a know-it-all, telling everyone what to do.

Josh glanced towards the woods below as he arrived at the shed. For a moment, he thought he'd seen a flash of light coming from the edge of the woods – but when he stared at it, there was nothing. Just a reflection from some wet leaves, he decided.

He turned off the MP3 player and started to open the padlock.

'Yes it's me,' he said. He glanced back at the woods. Still nothing. It must have just been his imagination.

'Just a week to go,' Josh told Reggae, as she jumped up to greet him. 'And you still have lots to learn. Let's go.'

Chapter 20

Josh felt unusually alert as he entered his English class the following day. For once, he was prepared – he'd listened to the play three times and even had a tutorial from Yvonne about it.

'As you all know,' Mrs Margolies began, 'this play takes place in two realms: in the human realm and in fairyland.' Josh recognised his teacher's joke – she knew full well most of the people in the class hadn't even glanced at the play. 'Today we're going to concentrate on fairyland. Who knows how Oberon seeks to punish Titania?'

Josh raised his hand eagerly. Mrs Margolies looked surprised, then annoyed.

'Josh, couldn't you have gone to the toilet during the break?'

'I don't want to go to the toilet,' he replied indignantly. 'I want to answer the question. Oberon punishes Titania by getting Puck to rub her eyes with a flower that will make her fall in love with the first person she sees.'

'That's right,' Mrs Margolies said, looking surprised. 'And why did he do that?'

'Well, he thought she'd fall in love with an animal in the forest, and be shamed by it. The idea was that this would make her give him the boy who's acting as her page.'

'Very good,' Mrs Margolies said with pleasure. 'And now, as you're doing so briliantly: why do you think Shakespeare introduced fairies into his story?'

Josh thought for a moment. He really liked the way the mischievous spirits threw everyone's plans into confusion. He remembered the way he'd thought Yvonne had dropped him for Eric. It was like for a moment, actually quite a few moments, everything he thought and felt had been turned upside down. But wasn't this a bit like what the spirits did in the play?

'I don't really know,' he said honestly. He heard a guffaw from Kearney and Angus, his sidekick.

'Quiet you two, or you'll get a detention,' said Mrs Margolies sharply. She turned back to Josh. 'You were saying . . .'

'The thing is, what you feel and think can just change, in a moment, for no good reason. I think Shakespeare has fairies in the story to show how random life is, how we think we know what we're doing, but we don't.'

Josh heard Kearney whisper to Angus, 'He'll find out how random life is . . .' Angus chuckled maliciously.

'Detention for both of you,' Mrs Margolies snapped. 'For today and tomorrow.'

Suddenly, Josh wondered if he'd been talking nonsense. But Mrs Margolies was looking at him differently.

'That's very good Josh. It's as good an explanation of Shakespeare's fairies as I've ever heard. Well done.'

Josh looked down at his desk in embarrassment. He couldn't ever remember a teacher talking to him like that. He looked up to find Yvonne's shining eyes on him. He mouthed 'thank you'. She blushed.

As the bell rang, Mrs Margolies said, 'Kearney, Angus and Josh, I want to see you before you leave.'

Josh put his copy of 'A Midsummer Night's Dream' in his rucksack and went up to the desk, where Mrs Margolies was scribbling detention notices for Kearney and Angus. They didn't seem bothered.

They went off, joking and laughing. Mrs Margolies pulled out a card from her drawer and started writing on it. 'Have you been studying?' she asked as she wrote.

'Yes,' he replied, 'And I'm getting help too.'

'But that answer didn't come from someone else . . .'

'No,' Josh said. Then he admitted. 'I don't know where it came from.'

'You're a smarter boy than you let on,' Mrs Margolies concluded, handing him a praise card. 'Show this to your uncle.'

Josh looked at the card, his first. It said 'for superior work and great insight into Shakespeare'. He rushed out of the class.

Yvonne was waiting for him outside. 'Look!' he said, showing her the card. She read it swiftly.

'You deserved it!'

'I just imagined I was talking to you.'

Yvonne didn't reply. Had he said something wrong? She turned and set off for their next class. But Josh would have sworn he heard her mutter, 'That's the nicest thing anyone ever said to me.'

* * *

Josh jogged towards home and Reggae's shed. It had been an amazing day and Mrs Margolies' words were on a repeating loop in his head. He couldn't wait to show her card to his uncle. His first praise card! And such an amazing one – 'insight into Shakespeare!' Uncle Calum would be surprised and pleased.

His head was so full of the day's events that he didn't really notice the shed door until he was almost upon it. It was slightly open. He must have forgotten to lock it after he took Reggae for her morning walk. He imagined Reggae seeing the open door and taking advantage of it, wandering off to explore. She'd be all right . . . He began to wonder where she might have gone.

That was when he noticed the padlock. It was on the ground. Unable to believe his eyes, he picked it up and stared at it. The shackle had been cut clean through. A chilly wind seemed to blow right through him.

He hadn't left the door ajar. Someone had broken it open. Josh felt numb. Someone with a big pair of bolt cutters. Who?

Operating his body mechanically, as if with a remote control, Josh opened the shed door and went in. The afternoon sun flooded into the dark space. Reggae's bed wasn't in its usual place, and it was upside down. Her toys were scattered over the wet side of the shed. She hadn't gone without a fight, he thought.

There was something dark and glistening on the floor. He knelt to have a closer look. He guessed what it was, but touched his finger to it to make sure. It was blood. Reggae – or someone – had been hurt in the struggle.

Josh tried to stand but the numbness he'd felt a moment earlier seemed to have drained into his legs – they just didn't seem to be working properly. He could only kneel, looking around at the shed, full of so many memories.

Who could have done this to him? His first thought was that his uncle might have noticed the lock on the shed . . . If he had, he might have cut it open.

But Josh couldn't imagine his uncle struggling with Reggae, fighting to remove her. His uncle was always incredibly kind to his animals. Josh knew if Uncle Calum had found a dog in a shed on his land he'd guess who it belonged to . . . And he'd have left her until Josh got home.

So it wasn't his uncle. Josh stared at the blood on the floor. Reggae wouldn't have fought like this unless someone was treating her cruelly . . .

A series of images flashed into his head. Dunham shouting at and striking his two young dogs.

Kearney catching him looking at the YouTube video in the library. Meeting Dunham in the small grocery store. Kearney at school showing off his binoculars. The glint of light from the woods as he opened the padlock.

Now Josh knew what had happened. Dunham *had* seen the dog food. He'd figured out Josh had a dog and had asked Kearney to find out where he kept it. He would've been pleased to do that, after Josh had shamed him. He must've followed Josh home after school, watched him from the woods with his binoculars . . . He'd seen him open the shed.

It would have been easy for Dunham to take Reggae while he was at school. Getting praised for the first time ever, he thought bitterly.

A tremor started in Josh's legs, and spread to his arms. What would Dunham do with her? He remembered Dunham in the valley, striking his dogs repeatedly. If Reggae bit him . . . Surely he wouldn't have killed her! Josh held his eyes shut as a wave of dismay and loss swept over him. The shed suddenly fell into darkness, as if a cloud covered the sun. No! It wasn't possible!

Josh struggled to get out from under the despair which threatened to swamp him. Reggae *couldn't* be dead. Dunham would've recognised she was a working dog. He wouldn't get rid of a working dog until he'd tried her out with some sheep. Especially when *his* dogs were so rubbish.

Josh had a scary thought. No one knew that Reggae belonged to Josh. Apart from Yvonne . . . If

Dunham saw what a good working dog she was, he might try to pass him off as his own!

At least, then, she'd still be alive.

Josh noted distantly his numbness was going. He managed to stand. He needed to think. There had to be *something* he could do.

Chapter 21

But as Josh wandered onto the commons, thinking seemed impossible. Everywhere he went reminded him of Reggae.

And everything that reminded him of her made him feel the hole in his world even more sharply.

But what was almost worse than her disappearance was the fact that *he* was to blame. If he hadn't interfered with Dunham in the valley, or been so careless in the grocery store, she'd be with him now. Even that carelessness wouldn't have been so bad if he'd realised that Dunham had seen the dog food . . . He could have hidden Reggae in a place where she'd never be discovered.

And then there were the binoculars . . . why hadn't he figured out why Kearney had brought them to school? Or that the flash of light in the forest had come from them?

Josh's feet were getting heavier by the moment. His mum had mattered more to him than anything in the world. He'd lost her. Now he'd lost Reggae. But this time it was worse, because it was *his* fault.

Josh's feet had taken him to the hills overlooking the secret valley, where he'd spent hours training Reggae. He looked down into it. Several small groups of sheep were grazing peacefully. Then Josh remembered the valley while he had watched, hidden, as Dunham's dogs charged into the sheep, biting, tearing chunks off their fleece, causing panic and distress to both the ewes and their young lambs . . .

Did he really regret stopping him?

No. He *couldn't* have done nothing. Yvonne was right. It just wasn't him.

But then it hit Josh: it *was definitely not him* to leave Reggae with a man like Dunham.

Up till now, it hadn't occurred to Josh that he could do anything to save Reggae – Dunham had just appeared too powerful, too *big* to go against. It would be like a five-year-old against the Incredible Hulk.

But remembering how he had confronted Dunham here, it didn't seem so impossible. Dunham *wasn't* the Incredible Hulk. Not even Iron Man. He was human. And he'd *never* expect Josh to have the courage to risk everything for his dog.

Suddenly, he didn't feel so helpless. Yes he'd made mistakes. But if he rescued Reggae . . . they wouldn't matter.

* * *

At the house, he changed out of his school uniform and left his praise note on the kitchen table for Uncle Calum to see as soon as he got home. He attached a Post-It note saying he was having a tutorial with Yvonne and would eat there.

It was already getting dark as Josh rounded the

equipment barn on the vet's farm. Josh automatically registered the vet's van was there – he was home.

The vet's dogs started to bark as he approached the front door. He gathered himself for a moment, then pressed the fire-engine-red doorbell. The door opened. It wasn't Yvonne. It was her father. Staring at the ground, Josh muttered 'Sorry to disturb you. I need to see Yvonne.' He started to sidle past him. He knew the time was coming when he had to have a proper conversation with the vet. But not now.

'Yvonne!' the vet called. He turned back to Josh. 'I hear you did really well in English today.'

Josh glanced up. The vet's face changed from his usual good humour to concern. For a moment, Josh wondered why. Then he realised his eyes must be puffy, and he quickly turned away. 'Thank you,' he whispered.

He heard someone getting up from the dinner table and then Yvonne's distinctive footsteps coming towards him down the hallway He looked up and could see her taking in the situation. Then he felt her hand on his back gently steering him towards the sitting room.

'You haven't finished dinner,' the vet said.

'I'll skip pudding,' Yvonne replied firmly. 'And I'll tidy up later.'

* * *

Once he'd realised he had to try to rescue Reggae, in the secret valley, all Josh could think was that he

137

had to talk to Yvonne. But now that he was here, he didn't know where to begin.

'What happened?' Yvonne had asked as soon as she'd sat Josh on the sofa. But all he could do was stare at the pattern on the brightly coloured Persian carpet on the floor.

Someone came into the room. Yvonne said 'ta', then handed him a glass of water. He drank it mechanically. 'My mum,' she explained. The vet must have told her he looked terrible.

'What happened?'

'She's gone,' Josh said, in a voice he hardly recognised. 'Someone took her.'

'. . . Reggae?'

Josh nodded. He looked up at her, feeling completely lost.

'When did you find out?'

'Just after school.'

'Why didn't you come straight here?'

It never occurred to him. He was used to dealing with things by himself.

After a pause, Yvonne said, 'We'll leave that for the moment . . . Tell me the whole story.'

'But you've got to tidy up . . .'

'We have plenty of time.'

* * *

Yvonne sat, listening carefully, until Josh finished his account. 'I can't believe Kearney would have helped his father do such a terrible thing.'

138

Josh didn't bother replying. The evidence spoke for itself.

'I've been to their place with my father a couple of times. But the last time was years ago,' she continued.

'Where did he keep his dogs?'

'In his front yard.'

'People don't usually move their kennels.'

'Do you really think he'd keep her in his kennel?'

'I don't even know if she's alive . . . But if she is, my guess is that he'd keep her close.'

'You won't get near the kennel without the dogs raising a huge racket,' Yvonne said quietly.

Josh had realised this while he walked on the commons. That's when he'd known he needed help.

'I'll need someone to provide a reason for the dogs' barking.'

'An accomplice,' Yvonne mused. Then she looked at Josh sharply. 'Me?'

He held her gaze. 'Who else could I ask?'

Josh could almost see her thinking. Of course she *wanted* to help him. But it would mean going against the biggest bully on the island. This wasn't something to do lightly. Josh had got into his bad books, and now he was paying the price.

After some minutes, Yvonne asked, 'Do you want to help me wash up?'

Josh nodded.

'Washing up helps me think,' Yvonne continued, rising to her feet. 'We have a lot of thinking to do.'

Josh followed Yvonne into the kitchen.

'And I suppose you haven't had anything to eat . . .'

* * *

Josh sat at the kitchen table, munching on cold chicken as Yvonne turned on her laptop.

'Here,' she said, indicating the screen. 'The Redlins' farm.'

It took Josh a moment to get his orientation. The photo was taken from above, probably from a satellite. 'That's brilliant!'

'We can make a map.'

'I can memorise it,' Josh said, his spirits rising.

'We need to anticipate everything,' Yvonne said. 'You won't have a second chance if you don't have everything you need with you.'

'I'll need to keep the dogs in the kennel quiet while I free Reggae,' Josh said, thinking aloud.

'My dad has tons of bones in his freezer. He won't miss a couple.'

'At least four,' Josh said. 'And we'll need to take them out tonight so they're completely defrosted.'

Yvonne nodded. 'What if Reggae isn't in the kennel? Or he's chained her up?'

Josh was sure Reggae *would* be in the kennel. But Yvonne was right. They should make plans in case she wasn't. And even if she was in the kennel, Dunham might have chained her to something.

'My uncle's got bolt cutters. I can borrow them.'

'Will they be strong enough?'

'They're old . . . But I'll sharpen them.'

Chapter 22

This was definitely a case of a problem shared, a problem halved, Josh thought as he headed home. They didn't have a proper plan yet. But they'd done a lot of thinking.

And he didn't feel so alone with it all. Which was nice, for a change.

To his surprise, his uncle, who often said (and usually practised) 'early to bed and early to rise' was still up when he got home. Not up in the sense of awake, but up in the sense of sitting, fully dressed, in his favourite armchair.

Josh tapped him gently on the shoulder. It took a moment for Calum to respond, but when he opened his eyes, they were already alert.

'I'm so proud of you,' he said warmly. 'I never got a comment from a teacher like that.'

'I was lucky.'

'Great insight into Shakespeare?' Calum recited from the card. 'It would take more than luck to deserve that . . . I'm sorry I can't give you a reward, like other parents,' he went on. 'But I just wanted you to know that I really appreciate the way you've buckled down and taken our conversation to heart.'

'Thank you.' It seemed an awfully long time since Mrs Margolies had written those comments. He wished he could tell Calum what was really on his mind. But that would mean admitting that he'd been lying. For months. How could he expect him to be sympathetic after that?

Still, he had to say *something* more than 'thank you'.

'Thanks for staying up too. We'd better get to bed.'

His uncle hesitated. He stood, suddenly looking old. Defeated.

What did he expect? Josh thought, defensively.

* * *

Calum had let him use the bathroom first, on the grounds that he had to get his rest so he could do well at school again the next day. He brushed his teeth mechanically. School was the last thing in Josh's thoughts. He was imagining how frightened Reggae must be.

An involuntary moan escaped him.

'Are you all right, Josh?' his uncle asked.

'I'm fine.'

Josh finished up and said good night again. Then he climbed the ladder to his room. He was aware of his uncle's eyes on him. The ladder seemed longer than usual.

And his bedroom darker. And emptier.

Josh was hardly aware of removing his clothes and climbing into bed. His only thoughts were of Reggae. How alone and cold she must feel.

Like *he'd* felt, when the police had come to his door that awful night.

He'd been asleep when the doorbell rang. He'd opened his eyes and had seen the mobile hanging over his bed, the one he and his mum had made, with planets and stars. When the bell rang a second time, he'd realised his mum wasn't home yet and he got up to answer it. His first thought, when he saw the two policemen, was that they'd come about the desk he'd written on at school.

They'd been awkward, two big men probably happier chasing a criminal with a gun than standing here on his doorstep.

'Can we speak to your father?'

'He's dead,' Josh told them.

'Is there another adult we could speak to?'

'Just my mum, but she's not here now. She's taking Charlene to the hospital.'

'Could we come in?'

'I'm not supposed to let strangers in.'

'That's generally good advice,' the bigger one had said.

The other said gently, '*We're* not really strangers,' and took out his police badge for Josh to look at.

Josh curled up on the worn sofa, still half asleep in his Transformer pyjamas. He wondered if he should offer them water, like his mum would have done.

The two policemen turned the armchairs around so that they faced him and not the telly. Then they sat, and looked at one another.

143

The smaller one said, 'Your mum has had an accident.'

Even then, Josh hadn't twigged. 'Is she hurt? Are you here to take me to see her?'

The big policeman asked, 'Do you have a relative living anywhere nearby?'

'What does that matter? She'll want to see *me*. Just take me there!'

'We can't do that.'

Then Josh had understood. It was as if suddenly he was far away from the living room and the two policemen, as if he'd been transported to outer space, to the planets in the mobile above his bed. He remembered thinking, as all the light in the room, in the world, vanished, this is what a black hole does . . .

* * *

Josh shivered in spite of the heat. How had he forgotten all that? He'd felt the world had come to an end then. But it hadn't, really.

He was still here. And in some ways, she'd come back to him, especially through her music. He reached over to the wooden box on the side of his bed and picked up the MP3 player Yvonne had given him. He turned it on. It was still tuned to the faint reggae programme he listened to late at night.

They were playing a song he remembered! It was his mother's 'fighting song'. The one she played (and sang, at the top of her lungs) before she went into 'battle' with teachers about Josh or council officers about their flat. They'd sing it together. He'd sing the chorus, 'Get up, stand up!' and she'd do the following verse. He listened to the radio. Yes, that was it! 'Don't give up the fight.' That's what she sang!

For a moment, Josh was lost in the memory. Then he thought, it's a sign they played that song just then.

He couldn't do a thing about his mother's accident. But he *wasn't* helpless now. He could fight. And he had a friend who would help him.

Chapter 23

Their bodies leant forward as they struggled to walk into the strong north-east wind. The drizzle that started when they left Yvonne's house had turned into a downpour. Josh's anorak protected his head and chest for the first ten minutes, but now the driving rain had forced its way through the hoodie's worn seams and waterproofing. His jeans were already completely soaked.

The wind blew Yvonne's umbrella inside out as soon as they hit the road. She just carried on without it.

As they caught their first sight of Dunham's dark house, silhouetted against the grey clouds in the distance, Josh said, 'Here's where I go.' He noticed the rain dripping steadily off Yvonne's glasses onto her nose and face, and her determined expression.

'Thank you,' he said. 'Whatever happens tonight.'

Yvonne touched him briefly on the arm. 'Good luck.'

Josh vaulted over the fence that marked the boundary to Dunham's property. He waved to Yvonne, and then jogged away. His heavy rucksack thudded rhythmically on his back. As he ran, he began to recognise buildings from the map he'd memorised.

It was unlikely anyone would be working outside in this weather, but he threaded his way through Dunham's farm buildings carefully just in case.

As he passed between two big barns, he suddenly stopped, startled, as he noticed the door to one of them was open. Was Dunham inside? Josh's first impulse was to run and hide. But then he realised he needed to know if someone was there. He couldn't afford to have Dunham stumble upon him while he was rescuing Reggae.

Josh crept up to the side of the open door, and tilted his head so that his ears were close. He wished he wasn't so tense, and tried to relax his breathing and shoulders. But after a few minutes, he realised the barn was empty and he started to breathe normally again. He headed for Dunham's house.

As he and Yvonne had planned, he ended up behind a red-roofed barn not far from the front door. He took out the mobile phone Yvonne had lent him and texted, 'I'm in position.'

*　　*　　*

As Yvonne waited in the pouring rain for Josh to text her, all the things that could go wrong with this hastily planned rescue wove through her mind: Reggae might not be where they expected. Dunham could answer the door. Kearney might have told his father that she was friends with Josh. And then there was all the lying she'd have to do: could she do it convincingly?

When the text finally arrived she was so tense, she fired off a response without thinking. 'What took you so long?' Josh's reply didn't help: 'Long story, later'. She pictured him alongside the barn, his face grim with determination. She was glad she was there to help him. And she hadn't felt this alive in ages!

She opened the garden gate. The dogs in the kennel started barking frantically. As she walked towards the door, she was sure she could see Josh moving towards the kennel out of the corner of her eye. But she didn't turn her head, in case someone in the house was watching her approach.

Water from the hood of her anorak dripped onto her face. She folded it back with her free hand and then rang the bell, praying that Dunham didn't answer. She'd prepared a little talk about how she was doing a sponsored walk for Children in Need, but she wasn't optimistic it would fool someone as suspicious as Dunham. The door started to open. Yvonne held her breath.

Relief flooded her body, as she recognised Mariella, Dunham's wife.

'Yvonne!' Mariella exclaimed. 'What a nice surprise! What brings you out on this dreadful night?'

'I'm going to do a sponsored walk. In support of Children in Need.'

* * *

Josh stayed behind the back of the kennel until he heard the door close. Yvonne had succeeded in the

149

first part of her mission – to enable him to get to the dogs.

The dogs were still barking frantically. They'd seen him running to hide behind their kennel. He had to get them to stop, otherwise the distraction Yvonne had provided would go to waste. He removed four meaty bones from his rucksack and, still crouching, stepped out from behind the kennel. The kennel was divided into two. There were two dogs on either side. Four dogs stared at him. Before they could react, he shoved two bones into each side of the kennel. There was a brief sound of growling, then the dogs went quiet. They couldn't eat and bark at the same time.

The two dogs nearest him were the ones he'd seen in the valley. They were looking up at him. 'Good boy,' he whispered, before they decided whether to bark or not. One left his bone and came up to the edge of the kennel. Josh stroked the side of his face. He could hardly believe a dog would leave a bone to get some affection. In a moment, the second dog was there. 'Good girl.'

But as Josh soothed the two dogs, a horrible realisation was hitting him. There were just four dogs in the kennel. And *none* of them was Reggae.

Could she really be . . . dead? His mind conjured up the scene – Dunham trying to drag her from her shed, her fighting back, biting him, drawing blood, and Dunham striking her hard, without thinking.

* * *

150

Yvonne took her time removing her boots as she sat at the kitchen table, as Mariella closed the door to the living room. With luck, Reggae would be in the kennel and her phone would buzz in a few moments.

When it didn't, Yvonne sighed inwardly. She'd have to do her 'talk'. She moved to the kitchen table, carrying her bag.

'Would you like some slippers?' Mariella asked. 'This floor is always freezing.'

Yvonne nodded and Mariella scurried off to a cupboard full of knitted slippers.

The slippers made a difference on the stone floor. 'Thanks,' Yvonne said. 'They're really lovely and warm. That was very thoughtful.'

Mariella blushed. 'It was nothing.'

'And such an interesting design. Where are they from?'

'My brother brought them from Canada.'

'I didn't know you had a brother in Canada,' Yvonne replied, attempting to keep the conversation going.

'He's not there anymore. He moved back to the island,' Mariella said, sitting down at the table. 'Tell me about your walk.'

Yvonne took out the papers and sponsorship form she'd prepared. Surely if Reggae had been in the kennel just outside the door, Josh would have texted her already. Which meant she wasn't . . . and that their plan wasn't working out the way they'd hoped. Now her job was to keep Mariella occupied as long as possible, to give Josh the best chance to find Reggae.

'It's 40 miles as the crow flies,' Yvonne said. 'Probably longer in reality.' Because Mariella had been really impatient when she talked about Children in Need, she'd cut that bit of her talk short and concentrated on her planned walk.

'That's quite a way,' Mariella interrupted.

'Would you like to sponsor me?'

'I know about long walks,' Mariella continued, as if Yvonne hadn't said anything.

'Do you?' Yvonne asked, as she took out her phone. She was sure she would have felt a text arrive, but she had to check. Nothing. And the clock on the phone showed her 'talk' had only taken a few minutes.

Where was Josh? And Reggae? What could she do now?

But Mariella was speaking to her. 'I've done lots of long walks, five days, even a week. So you're fortunate to be talking to me, even though your walk will only take two or three days. I know as much as anyone on the island about long-distance walking. Walking that far is a serious matter,' she continued. 'Blisters . . . that's your major concern. They can stop you in your tracks.'

'Really?' Yvonne said. She was beginning to realise that the reason Mariella hadn't wanted to hear about Children in Need was because *she* wanted to talk about the walk. And that she'd closed the door to the living room because she was starved of conversation. All Yvonne needed to do was listen, and provide some encouragement.

'Vaseline and thick socks. They're the key to stopping blisters. And well broken-in shoes . . . Do you know about breaking in shoes?'

'Not anything like enough,' said Yvonne, trying to look interested.

'Well,' said Mariella. 'Shoes are a very big topic!'

Yvonne began to relax. All she had to do was let Mariella go on.

It was then that the door to the living opened. And Kearney entered.

* * *

Josh sat listening to the dogs gnawing through the bones he'd given them, paralysed by crippling thoughts, which seemed to be on a permanent loop in his head.

'This was your brilliant plan? Look for Reggae in the kennel by Dunham's front door? What a loser. You don't deserve a dog like Reggae! Or a friend like Yvonne. You're just sitting there, useless and stupid, as she risks everything to help you. Useless and stupid. That's you.'

Through the window, Josh saw Kearney come into the kitchen. For a moment, he almost welcomed this, as it would bring his agony to an end. But then he thought about Reggae, lost and hopeless. She trusted him.

Then the tune popped into his head. 'Get up, stand up!' His mother's fighting song again! 'Stand up for your rights!' *She* didn't want him to give up.

His brain shifted up a gear. He began to think. Okay, he'd been wrong about the kennel. Yvonne had always said Dunham was too devious to put Reggae there.

He had to think like Dunham. And he didn't have any time to waste.

* * *

Yvonne forced herself to smile.

'I thought I heard your voice,' Kearney said. 'What are you doing here?'

'I'm going to do a sponsored walk. For Children in Need. I never knew your mum knew so much about walking.'

In Yvonne's eyes, Mariella seemed to grow, like a plant being watered.

'She likes nothing better than to set out on a rainy day with her rucksack and a thermos,' Kearney said proudly, putting his hand on his mother's shoulder.

Now Yvonne imagined Mariella blossoming.

'I don't remember doing anything about fund-raising for Children in Need at school,' Kearney said suspiciously.

'It's not a school project,' Yvonne replied quickly. 'I've been thinking about it for a while.'

As soon as she said this, Yvonne kicked herself mentally. That was a terrible way to put it, because it would make Kearney wonder why she was doing it today.

Kearney looked at her searchingly. Yvonne fought to keep calm. When she'd agreed to do this, she hadn't thought about how it would involve lying to people she knew.

'I see,' Kearney said, nodding to himself.

Yvonne had a terrible feeling he did see.

'I really miss walking home with you,' Kearney said.

Yvonne tried to hide her dismay. She could see Kearney was thinking how Josh had taken his place. And how Josh was no friend of his . . .

Then Kearney surprised her.

'Josh was in a really bad way today, wasn't he?' Kearney continued. 'He looked like a scarecrow with the stuffing knocked out.'

Now there was no doubt. He knew. Yvonne's heart sank. What was Kearney going to do? And why hadn't Josh texted? Where *was* he?

* * *

Josh crouched by the kennel and tried to think like Dunham. Where was the least likely place you'd put a stolen sheepdog?

With sheep? Josh smiled grimly at the thought.

155

You didn't keep sheep inside a building. But what about other animals? You wouldn't keep most Borders with animals – they'd bark and harry them. But Reggae wasn't your typical Border. She'd been trained to be quiet. Would Dunham have realised that?

He would have! Because Reggae wouldn't have barked, even while he cut off the padlock to his shed . . . She may have created a racket when Dunham tried to grab her . . . but Dunham would have guessed it was safe to keep her with animals.

Josh felt a surge of excitement. Okay, he said to himself, you've thought like Dunham, where's Reggae?

Josh remembered the barn with the open door. There were three calves there. Could Reggae be there?

He hoicked his rucksack onto his back and took a final look at the kitchen. Oh no!

* * *

The door from the living room burst open and Dunham entered the kitchen, his face red with anger.

He spoke to his wife sharply. 'I've been waiting for that cup of tea you promised fifteen minutes ago!'

Mariella seemed to shrink visibly. She jumped up and scuttled over to the kettle. 'I'm so sorry. I got involved in a conversation . . . It'll just be a minute.'

Even though she knew it was stupid, Yvonne tried to make herself as small as possible. Kearney had turned his face away from his father. But before he'd moved, Yvonne had registered how upset he seemed. Was it because he realised she was helping Josh?

Dunham turned to leave. It seemed he had been placated by the way Mariella had jumped to attend to him. Yvonne's shoulders began to relax as she began to hope he hadn't noticed her.

Too soon. Before he reached the door, Dunham swivelled around and faced her. 'The vet's daughter,' he said, like a spider who had just noticed a fly caught in his web. 'And to what do we owe this visit?'

'She's doing a sponsored walk for Children in Need.' Mariella answered swiftly, while reaching for a tin of biscuits.

'Did I ask you anything?' Dunham said.

Mariella hunched over the little saucepan. 'No,' she said, almost inaudibly.

Dunham took a step towards Yvonne. He towered above her in the tiny kitchen. Kearney, who now seemed in control of himself, turned to face his father.

Dunham was looking at her expectantly, but Mariella had already answered his question. What was she supposed to say? Especially when she could almost see Dunham's suspicious mind making links between Reggae, Josh and her.

'I'm going to walk from the north end of the island to the south,' Yvonne said, trying to smile brightly.

'When's this "walk" happening?'

'In ten days.'

'Strange then, it was so urgent to sign us up you had to go out on a night like this . . .'

'He doesn't know anything,' Yvonne told herself. 'He's just fishing.'

* * *

Josh knew he had to hurry. It took just a few minutes to get to the barn with the calves. He removed his torch from the rucksack and switched it on. The light highlighted the drops of falling rain. Holding his breath, he entered through the open door. The three calves looked at him, blinking in the bright light. But as he scanned the rest of the barn, he saw Reggae wasn't there. He'd been wrong.

His shoulders slumped. He *hadn't* figured out how Dunham would think . . . in fact, every single idea he'd had about this rescue mission had been wrong. He was useless.

* * *

Yvonne watched as Mariella finished preparing Dunham's cup of tea. Then she brought it over to him and stood awkwardly by his side. Yvonne noticed she'd put several biscuits on the side of the saucer.

When Dunham didn't move to take the cup, Mariella asked, 'Would you like me to take it into the living room for you?'

Dunham gave her a shark-toothed smile. 'I think I'll pass some more time with our visitor . . .' He left his wife holding the cup of tea and, ignoring both her and Kearney, focused on Yvonne. 'I've seen you walking with Calum's boy, haven't I?'

Involuntarily, her hand went to the mobile on the table. Dunham noticed.

'Waiting for a call?'

* * *

Josh thought even James Bond would have trouble keeping a secret from Dunham. Yvonne didn't have a chance. It would just take seconds before Dunham saw through her. And a few seconds more before he knew why she was there . . .

'Get up, stand up. Don't give up the fight.'

He couldn't stop now. Reggae needed him. Josh stepped out into the driving rain.

He didn't have time to search every one of Dunham's farm buildings. Why didn't he just call Reggae? The sound of his voice would be muffled by the downpour. But what would be the point? Josh had taught her never to bark.

'Don't give up the fight.'

'Reggae,' he called out. He was shocked at the sound of his voice – it sounded cracked and desperate. He turned to face the farm buildings at his back, and called out again. 'Reggae!'

* * *

Yvonne's brain seemed to step up a gear. Dunham's voice had been gentle, but she knew there was a

159

threat behind it. It was the same bullying tone he'd used with Mariella. She had to stop being scared and start thinking strategically. Maybe she couldn't prevent him from discovering Josh, but she wasn't going to make it easy for him.

'My dad's out at a farm nearby. He said he'd ring on his way home, in case I wanted a lift.'

'He knows you're here, then . . .'

Yvonne seemed to be digging a deeper hole, and not only for herself. 'Of course.'

Dunham looked at her sceptically. 'I'm not a big believer in coincidence,' he said. He turned to Kearney. 'Go check on our recent arrival.'

Yvonne forced her face to remain still. She wasn't going to let this man intimidate her. 'Do you have an early calf, then?'

Dunham looked disconcerted, as if, for a moment, he was questioning his reading of the situation.

Kearney smiled fondly at Yvonne. Mariella, tired of waiting, put Dunham's cup of tea down heavily on the kitchen counter. 'I didn't know we had an early calf . . .'

'I don't tell you everything, woman.' Then he turned to Kearney. 'Move!' he ordered.

Yvonne knew most people would have flinched at the force of Dunham's voice. But Kearney stayed completely still. Then he gathered himself and stood just a bit taller. What was he going to do?

'There's no need to talk to Mum that way.'

Dunham glared at Kearney, who stared right back at him. They were both the same height, Yvonne realised, though Dunham was much the more imposing presence.

'We'll talk about this later. I asked you to do something.'

'You didn't "ask", actually.'

Yvonne sensed how much courage it was taking for Kearney to speak to his father this way.

'I will check. In a couple of minutes,' he continued. 'But I need to ask Yvonne about our geography homework first.'

Dunham's face flushed with colour.

Mariella came in quickly. 'I didn't know you had homework . . .'

Yvonne silently thanked Mariella for joining in. What would Dunham do now?

* * *

Josh stood in the rain, turning in a circle. Listening for Reggae's bark. He couldn't hear a thing. Just the sound of the rain pounding on the metal barn roofs.

What did he have to lose? Life without Reggae would be just too bleak to face.

'REGGAE!' he shouted.

Still nothing.

Then he heard it. Two short barks. Coming from the building right next to the one with the calves. Was it really her? Josh charged over and opened the door. There were four cows in pens here. And Reggae, chained to the wall up on the other side of

161

the barn. Dunham *had* kept her with his animals!

She leapt up onto his chest, and licked his face, again and again. He hugged her tight, fighting back tears.

He removing his uncle's bolt cutters from his rucksack. The edges of their blades gleamed. He'd sharpened them when he was supposed to be at lunch. 'Let's get you out of here.'

* * *

Yvonne kept an eye on Dunham as she told Kearney about their homework. 'Mr Eldon asked us to draw a map showing the effects of the glaciers across Scotland and the islands. It's a bit complicated. Do you want to write it down?'

Kearney nodded, and slowly walked over to the telephone where there was a pad of paper and a pen. Then he returned to the kitchen table and sat down. Dunham watched this movement with barely concealed rage. Yvonne worried about the price Kearney would pay for his help.

Kearney started writing. 'A map showing the effects of the glaciers.'

'We need to show which lochs were formed by them.'

Kearney scribbled on the notepad.

Yvonne continued, 'And which mountain ranges are glacial as opposed to volcanic. Also the U-shaped valleys that were carved out.'

'I hate these geography projects,' Kearney said, as he finished writing. He looked up and gave Yvonne a soft look. He then glanced over to his father, who was standing with his arms crossed, fuming.

Kearney turned back to Yvonne. 'Have you done it already?'

Yvonne nodded, recognising Kearney was trying to give them a few more precious moments, in spite of his father's anger. How brave he was!

* * *

The chains that were holding Reggae were brand new. And the links were too close together to cut them one at a time. Josh struggled to bring the arms of the bolt cutter together. He'd never tried to cut anything that was so hard.

Maybe they were made of some new kind of metal . . . Josh hoped his uncle's old bolt cutter was up to the task.

Reggae sat, keeping her liquid eyes on his face.

Josh's muscles felt close to snapping as he strained to force his arms together, closing the bolt cutter. What if he wasn't able to do it? What if he failed so close to his goal?

He loosened his grip, put down the bolt cutter and stretched his arms out in every direction. Then he picked up the cutter again. It was now or never. Yvonne couldn't keep Dunham away forever.

He fastened the cutters around the chain in the same place, noting with dismay that he hadn't even dented it with his last try. It didn't matter, he told himself. This time he was going to succeed.

He pulled the chain up so that he could stand, and get the full force of his shoulders behind his arms. Then keeping his eyes on Reggae, he forced his arms together. Nothing happened. The chain seemed break-proof.

Josh knew he was almost out of time. He put everything he had into the bolt cutter. For a moment, he wasn't sure it would be enough.

'CRAAACK!' The old bolt cutter came apart in his hands. A wave of despair swept over Josh. He'd failed.

Then he realised the chain was also lying in pieces. His last supreme effort had cracked the bolt cutter and the chain *together*.

Reggae sat quietly, waiting to be released, her trust in Josh complete.

Josh felt like crying. He took out Yvonne's phone from his trousers.

*   *   *

Yvonne felt her phone vibrate in her hand. She didn't dare look at the message. But she prayed it was Josh. But first she had to answer Kearney.

'I found the map on a school website. I'll email it to you.'

Dunham had heard the phone buzz too. He gave Kearney an angry look. 'Your father,' he said to Yvonne, in a flat voice.

Yvonne nodded.

Kearney rose. 'I'll check on the recent arrival now.'

'I'll come with,' Dunham decided suddenly.

Yvonne didn't like the sound of that. She stood, and went over to Mariella. She gave her a warm hug. 'Thanks for the donation, the cup of tea, and the advice. I may need to ask you a few more questions about shoes.'

'You can call any time,' Mariella responded equally warmly.

Yvonne nodded curtly to Dunham.

'Remember me to your father,' he said ominously.

'I will,' Yvonne replied, smiling brightly.

Kearney and his father left the house at the same time as Yvonne. Dunham picked up a long case. It took a moment for Yvonne to register what it was. A shotgun! She knew she only had a minute or two until he and Kearney discovered Reggae was gone. Then Dunham would know her father wasn't picking her up. But she forced herself to walk normally, at least until they were out of sight.

Then, leaving the gate wide open, she ran, tearing down the road as fast as she could.

Josh had arranged to meet her by the bus shelter. As she ran towards it, he stepped out from behind it. Reggae was by his side, and she wagged her tail furiously at the sight of Yvonne.

'We don't have time for greetings,' she gasped. 'Dunham will be right behind me. He had a gun.'

They heard a loud crash from behind them. The direction of the barn.

Josh asked incredulously. 'A gun?'

Yvonne nodded.

Josh started to run down the verge alongside the road. Yvonne followed, just a few steps behind him. Reggae raced ahead.

'We've got to get off the road,' Yvonne wheezed. She wasn't used to running. 'He'll think of his car soon.'

As if to confirm her thought, they heard shouting from the farm.

Yvonne looked ahead on the road. There were ditches filled with water on both sides. Behind them were steep embankments, topped by wire fences. How were they going to get off?

Yvonne watched as Josh raced ahead, Reggae keeping pace with him. They disappeared around the bend of the road.

Yvonne forced air in and out of her lungs. Even just breathing was painful. But she knew she couldn't stop running. They had a minute or two at most to get off the road.

As she rounded the curve of the road, she heard Josh.

'Up here!'

He was at the top of a small rise above the road, a break in the high embankment. His rucksack was on the ground and he seemed to be wearing some kind of gloves.

Yvonne stumbled through the ditch, glad, for the first time, she was wearing boots. As she laboured to reach the top, she saw Josh lift the barbed wire with his gloved hand. As she reached the top, she saw a car's lights illuminating the road behind them.

Josh yanked her through the fence and down to the ground. Then he dived down next to her.

Dunham's car rounded the bend, and sped on.

Chapter 24

The smell of damp clothes permeated the vet's barn. Josh's soaking trousers, shirt and socks were spread out over the hay bales. Yvonne had brought him one of her dad's shirts and a pair of old jeans. All their clothes had been a mess by the time they'd reached home. She'd changed too, into jeans and a hoodie.

Josh had borrowed one of her father's dog brushes. He had just started to get the tangles out of Reggae's fur when he discovered the first of the cuts. At first, he could hardly believe it. Then he found the second cut, and the third. There were bruises too. Everywhere.

'I need some antiseptic,' he said to Yvonne. 'Something that won't sting.'

While Yvonne went to get something from her father, Josh washed Reggae tenderly with a tub of warm water. He felt awful that Reggae had had to experience such a cruel man in charge of her, even for a day. And more than that, he was furious with Dunham. There would have been no cause for such treatment. Reggae would have done everything he asked.

When Yvonne returned, Josh dabbed antiseptic into the cuts, talking softly to Reggae as he did.

'It's all over, girl. Nothing like that will ever happen to you again.'

After he was sure he'd treated all the cuts, he

touch-dried Reggae with a towel, just as he had a year earlier, when he'd found her by the river.

As soon as he was finished, Reggae licked his face and rolled over onto her back. 'You want a tummy tickle? You deserve it.'

Josh couldn't quite take in that he had her back. As he stroked her and blew raspberries into her tummy, he started to tremble.

Yvonne noticed immediately. 'What's wrong?'

'I must have got a chill,' Josh said, feeling foolish.

Yvonne found a heavy blanket and draped it over his shoulder.

But the shivering got worse.

'I've seen you out in the winter cold with just a T-shirt,' Yvonne said.

'. . . what if I hadn't found . . .' Josh couldn't finish the sentence. His juddering continued. Like a tractor running with dirty diesel.

'You're white as a sheet,' Yvonne said, bringing him another blanket. 'Shock.'

A fresh bout of shivering hit him. He realised he'd felt cold, no, deep frozen, inside, ever since he'd found the broken padlock outside Reggae's shed. As usual, Yvonne was right.

He hated being the centre of attention. Especially for shaking and shivering. And he still hadn't heard what had happened inside the house.

'I saw Kearney in the kitchen. That must have been really difficult for you . . .'

'It was scary,' Yvonne admitted. 'But not half as scary as when Dunham came in . . .'

'I saw him,' Josh said. 'That's when I thought it was all over. What happened?'

Yvonne told him the whole story.

Kearney helped? It didn't make sense. 'Are you sure Kearney knew?'

Yvonne nodded. 'Kearney's not how you think. He was shocked by how you looked yesterday.'

Josh found it difficult to believe he'd care.

'I think it made a difference that you apologised,' Yvonne continued. 'It was one of the bravest things I've ever seen. I don't want to think . . . what Dunham will do.'

Josh remembered how hard it had been for him to stand up to Dunham when he'd seen his dogs hurting Calum's sheep. It must have been ten times harder for Kearney to stand up to his own father.

'I may have got him wrong,' Josh had to admit.

Yvonne seemed pleased. 'Maybe you two can become friends.'

That was going a bit far. But he wasn't going to say that to Yvonne now. Not after she'd risked so much to help him. He switched the subject.

'You're just amazing,' he said. 'I loved how you came up with geography homework. How did you stay so cool?'

'I didn't *feel* very cool,' Yvonne admitted. 'But with Kearney helping I didn't feel so alone . . . Where are you going to keep Reggae the next couple of days?' Yvonne asked.

'In my room,' Josh replied. He'd already decided that this was the only place he'd feel certain Reggae was safe. It was only three days until the Gathering. He could smuggle her in and out when his uncle wasn't around. She'd have no problem controlling her bladder now. And she knew better than to make any noise.

Josh looked at Yvonne. She was looking down, playing with the ends of her hair, which was still damp from the rain. Without her, he'd have lost Reggae forever.

'Look, I . . . erm . . . Thanks for everything,' Josh said awkwardly.

Yvonne picked up Reggae's half-eaten bone and threw it at Josh. Reggae leapt up and caught it in mid-air.

She laughed with surprise. 'You have no idea, Josh, what a pain it is being the vet's daughter . . . Everyone knows me! I always have to be so *good* . . . Tonight, it was like I was helping in a bank robbery. It was great!'

Chapter 25

Josh woke up with the warm sun on his face and the sound of gentle breathing by his side. He leaned over and rubbed his nose against Reggae's. Her eyes opened. He could have sworn she smiled. Well anyway, she licked his face.

It had been a rough night. Reggae's frantic cries woke Josh several times. Her breathing was rapid and her legs were trying to run. Josh held her close and woke her with soft words. It wasn't hard to imagine what she was having nightmares about. Each time, it took ages for her breathing to slow down. Afterwards, she'd cuddled up to him even closer before going back to sleep.

Josh checked the alarm clock and pulled on his school uniform. 'Stay,' he ordered. 'I'll check if it's safe for you to come down and pee.' He climbed down the ladder.

When he returned, he was surprised to see Reggae had already climbed into his rucksack, for her trip down the ladder.

*   *   *

He met up with Yvonne near the tree where they'd rescued the baby bird.

'Sleep okay?' Yvonne asked.

Josh explained about Reggae's nightmares.

'Poor pup,' she exclaimed. 'At least she had you next to her to comfort her . . . What's on today?' she asked.

'Revising,' Josh replied. 'We've got two days to go over all the commands she's learned and make sure she's not forgotten anything.'

'And my father?' Yvonne prompted.

'I'll talk to him,' Josh said grimly.

'When?'

'I said, I'll talk to him,' Josh snapped. He regretted it immediately. How could he be angry with her after all she'd done for him?

'Keep your shirt on,' Yvonne said, rolling her eyes. 'It's not my fault you've left it until absolutely the last minute. One thing that might help: I heard my dad talking on the phone to someone about the fact they don't have enough trained dogs this year . . .'

'Ta,' said Josh, still embarrassed by his outburst. Suddenly, out of the corner of his eye, he saw someone approaching. Kearney. He shifted his weight from one leg to the other, dreading the conversation ahead.

There was an odd quality to Kearney's walk. It was as if he were trying not to move his chest or arms.

'Thanks,' Kearney said.

They started towards school, Josh and Kearney flanking Yvonne.

'What happened last night after I went?' Yvonne asked.

'He went mad when he discovered she'd gone.

We chased you in the car, but you'd disappeared. It turns out he'd been planning to pretend she was his at the Gathering.'

'What about you?'

'The usual,' Kearney said dismissively. 'I can take it.' Josh saw him wince as he stepped over a branch on the path. *That* was why he was holding himself so weirdly. He was in pain.

He needed to say *some*thing. 'Thank . . .'

'I didn't do it for you,' Kearney barked, interrupting him.

'Still . . .' Josh persisted.

'Shut. Your. Face.'

Josh felt both disappointed and relieved. Nothing had really changed.

'Kearney!'

Kearney gave Yvonne a sharp, hurt look. 'And thank you too!' he said sarcastically, taking out his mobile. 'I'm going to wait for my *friends*.'

Yvonne gestured for Josh to go on. He did. After a bit, he glanced back and saw her speaking insistently to Kearney. He had his arms folded across his chest and was looking away.

Josh felt for Kearney. He was proud. Maybe too proud. But, Josh had to agree, he had a right to feel it today – not many people would have stood up to Dunham like he had.

He started towards school. Yvonne caught up to him a few minutes later. Her face was sad. Josh felt for her. She'd really believed Kearney had changed. That the two of them could become friends. It was a nice dream.

Chapter 26

Josh stopped in front of the familiar door. He reminded himself of what he wanted to say, and how he wanted to appear calm and composed, adult. He told himself the vet was an ordinary human being. Then he pushed the bright red button. As he waited, he wiped the beads of sweat from his forehead with the sleeve of his hoodie.

Yvonne answered. When she saw Josh she smiled. 'You didn't half leave it till the last minute. Come on, then. He's in his study.'

She led the way. At the door, she said, 'Dad, Josh wants to speak to you.' Then she gave Josh an encouraging smile and retreated.

'Come in.'

Josh entered. The vet's study was lined with dark wood bookshelves filled with well-worn books. If possible, this made Josh feel more daunted. His uncle's house had one small shelf of books, mostly ancient Reader's Digest Condensed ones.

The vet was sitting at a large, dark, wooden desk. It had piles of paper covering most of its surface. He was wearing glasses and was poring over a piece of paper with names on it.

Josh had spent a great deal of time over the past couple of months thinking about this conversation:

what he should say, how to respond to the vet's objections. 'Mr White, I'd like to put my name down for the Gathering. I'll be coming with my sheepdog, Reggae.'

The vet's eyes smiled. 'I think that's the first complete sentence you've ever said to me, Josh.'

That wasn't in the script he'd rehearsed.

Involuntarily he looked down at the ground. No! he told himself. You have to look him in the eye. He did.

'I'm serious about the Gathering, Mr White.'

The vet looked at Josh, then took off his reading glasses, polished them on his shirt and laid them on the desk.

'You're big for your age, Josh. But you're in Yvonne's class at school.'

'I know I'm only twelve,' Josh blurted out, forgetting his carefully planned speech. 'But I'm able to do a man's work and I have a Border collie who is a natural dog and who will do a great job with the sheep, and we want to do the fank too.'

'We'd be pleased to have you help out.'

Josh shook his head vigorously. 'I don't want to "help out!"'

'You're wanting . . . to do this as an adult?'

Josh's forehead was wet with sweat. His whole plan to keep Reggae depended on the vet saying 'yes', and getting a share of the money that was earned by the crofters who participated. 'Yes, sir. Please give me a chance. My dog is special.'

'Yvonne never mentioned a dog. Who trained it?'

'I saved her from the river last year. And I trained her myself. She's a secret dog.'

'I see,' the vet said. Like Yvonne, he seemed to understand a great deal more than was said. 'So you've got a lot riding on being part of the Gathering and fank.'

'Yes, Mr White.'

'You don't have to call me Mr White. Neill will do.'

'I'll try,' Josh said.

Neill stared into the upper right corner of the room. 'The other men will tease you, Josh. Both as a newcomer and as a boy.'

'I know,' Josh said. It was the way the crofters got the measure of someone new. He knew they didn't mean any harm by it. They just wanted to know what people were made of. Their lives were hard and they needed to know who they could count on.

Josh wasn't looking forward to it. But he knew he had to go through it – for Reggae's sake. He'd have to give as good as he got.

'We've had boys help out, in the pens and on the field. But never do the full two weeks.'

'I'm not afraid of hard work. And I've heard they're short of dogs this year.'

The vet looked at Josh suspiciously. As if he was trying to figure out how he knew that . . .

'Yvonne,' Neill had answered his own question.

Josh stayed silent. He'd made all his arguments. He prayed they were enough.

'*No one* knows about your dog?' the vet asked. 'Not even Calum?'

Josh shook his head.

Neill frowned. 'Are you sure this is the way you want to do it?'

He was asking whether Josh really wanted to keep his dog a secret from his uncle until after the Gathering. He nodded.

Neill grimaced. 'I hope you know what you're doing, Josh . . . I'll put you on the list,' he said, after a long pause. 'But it's not me you have to impress.'

'I'll take my chances with the crofters.' Josh said. Most of them knew Calum, and would give him a chance. Except for Dunham, who was definitely now a mortal enemy.

'Thank you, Mr White.'

The vet rose from his chair. Josh could see it was painful for him to move.

'My daughter talks a lot about you.'

'She's my best friend,' Josh replied 'Thanks again. For giving me a chance. You won't regret it.'

Chapter 27

The early morning sun flooded Josh's room. No point in trying to get back to sleep. They had to get going, before Calum got up. He roused Reggae and carried her down the ladder. She waited eagerly as he opened a tin of dog food.

Her familiar gobbling noise filled the room. He sat at the dark kitchen table and started to write.

'Dear Uncle Calum,' he began. 'There's something I should have told you and I'll do it tonight but I'm going to help with the Gathering today . . .'

He shook his head, crumpled it up and started again.

'Dear Uncle Calum, I'm really sorry about this but I've kept a secret from you . . .'

He crumpled this one up too, and it followed the first into his pocket. Somehow, writing this note seemed to make what he'd done – keep Reggae a secret from Calum – more real. He remembered the vet's question, 'Are you sure you want to do it this way?'

Now, too late, he wasn't sure . . .

Reggae had finished her breakfast and was looking up at him expectantly. If he didn't hurry, his uncle would wake up before they got away. He didn't have time for doubts now. He had to follow the plan.

He scribbled:

> Dear Uncle Calum,
> I'm going to help with the Gathering today. I'll explain everything tonight.
> Love,
> Josh

Then he grabbed his rucksack and fled the house, Reggae on his heels.

* * *

Just ahead was the valley where they'd started their training. Reggae waited patiently for him to catch up.

Josh stopped and stroked the side of her face. Reggae looked expectantly down into the valley.

'Not today,' he told her, shaking his head. 'Today is the real thing.' He glanced at his watch.

'We need to go.' He could feel his reluctance to leave the valley: familiar, like a well-worn – and well-loved – pair of trainers.

Suddenly, Josh knelt down and hugged Reggae tight. 'This has been the best year of my life. Because of you.'

Reggae licked his face. Josh's nerves had passed, like a storm. He was glad they'd stopped here. Away from the meeting point.

* * *

'That's where it all starts,' Josh said, pointing down from the hill to the flat area below. The now empty pens for the sheep were set out loosely in a semi-circle, around where people were beginning to gather. Beyond them was the field where battered Land Rovers and other well-worn 4×4s were parked.

Josh couldn't see faces from this distance, but he recognised the vet's cowboy hat and distinctive hobbling walk. Yvonne was with him, carrying a clipboard.

Dunham would be there, if not now, soon. Josh hadn't seen him since he'd rescued Reggae. He'd have to be brave.

'Ready?' he asked his dog. Reggae wagged her tail.

Feeling like Luke Skywalker going to the showdown with Darth Vader, Josh started down the hill.

* * *

Halfway down, he recognised Mr Sampson, his history teacher. He had a dog with him, a bearded collie. Josh went over to say hello.

'Josh,' the teacher exclaimed. 'I didn't expect to see you here.'

'I didn't expect to see you! I didn't know you had a dog,' Josh replied.

'Bobby belongs to my brother on the mainland. I always bring him over for the Gathering. It's a good excuse to spend my day outdoors. And today,

183

for a change, the weather has cooperated,' he said, looking up at the bright blue sky. 'And the young border . . . is she yours?'

Josh glanced down at Reggae, who was anxiously looking from Mr Sampson's dog to the others around her. With a shock, Josh realised that Reggae had never been around other dogs. He didn't know how she'd behave.

Why hadn't he anticipated this? He'd *known* there would be other dogs at the Gathering . . . why hadn't he found a way to give Reggae some experience of being around them?

'Is something wrong?' Mr Sampson was asking.

Josh shook his head. Bobby was drifting closer to Reggae, to have a friendly sniff. Josh watched with trepidation. Reggae growled deep in her throat.

'No Reggae,' he said quickly, bending over to grab her collar. He hurriedly pulled the lead from his rucksack and attached it. Josh looked around him, feeling sick with worry now. More and more men and their dogs were arriving. What if Reggae decided every dog was her enemy? How could he have overlooked this?

'All gather round,' the vet was shouting. 'We need to get started. Long day ahead.'

Josh bent and held Reggae's collar as the area around the vet become tightly crowded with men and dogs. Kneeling made him feel even smaller, a boy amongst men. Every time Reggae started to growl, he pulled her collar tighter. But he couldn't do this all day. She had to be free to roam.

A man Josh didn't know said, 'She's an aggressive little one, isn't she?'

Josh's first impulse was to defend Reggae. He stood up. Even though the man wasn't taller than him, he felt like a bamboo stem next to a stout oak. He searched for something to say. Then he realised the man was smiling. He'd meant it as a compliment.

'She's not used to having so many other dogs around,' Josh replied.

The man bent over and tickled Reggae under the ear. 'Borders can be like that. Lovely dog. Young, isn't she?'

'Just over a year.' Josh said.

'Calum's boy?' the man asked, trying to place Josh.

From his tone of voice, the man was obviously fond of Calum. Josh remembered the note he'd left for his uncle. He imagined Calum finding it, wondering what it meant . . .

He nodded. 'Josh,' he said, extending his hand.

The man shook his hand firmly. 'Hamish.'

The vet shouted, so that he could be heard over the crowd and the dogs barking and growling. 'Gather round.'

Josh watched as Yvonne handed her father the clipboard and pointed to a place on the paper.

The vet continued. 'Three dogs for each hill, top, middle and bottom. We'll start at the Hay's End and drive them to the pens here at Romesdal. I've got the assignments here. Pay attention. I'm not going to read these out again.'

185

Josh's name was the first on the list. Without thinking, he shouted out, 'Present.' A number of the men chuckled. He'd answered as if he were at school! Everyone was looking at him. He wished he could disappear

The vet had put him on the Old Road. He listened to see who he'd be working with. Mr Sampson! The two of them would be responsible for driving the sheep who'd come off the hill down the road towards the pen.

Who would be on the hills around them, driving the sheep down to the road? His heart sank as he heard the vet announce Dunham's name.

Why did he have to put him together with Dunham? Then Josh realised Yvonne wouldn't have told her father what had happened, because she would have had to admit her part in the rescue.

*   *   *

'We'll start here,' Dunham said, taking charge of the group of eight. He stared at Josh. 'Mr White may think it's a joke to have a boy pretending to be a man. I don't.' Reggae growled at Dunham. Josh held her collar tight.

A second man agreed. 'The vet's taking the piss, giving us a toddler and his pet. And on the road too!'

Encouraged, Dunham went further. 'I don't want to see any of the ewes I've driven down to the road wandering off. Otherwise, your Gathering will end today.'

Josh knew no one could help him now. He'd betrayed how young he was once. He couldn't afford to again. He forced himself to look Dunham in the eye. He took a deep breath and drew himself up to his full height. 'I know I, and my dog, are young,' he said. 'But I've always heard crofters judge people by the weight they carry.'

Dunham flushed. He didn't like Josh talking back to him. An older man, who seemed familiar to Josh somehow, didn't say anything, but smiled encouragingly at Josh.

'I like his spirit,' one of the other crofters said approvingly.

And another echoed. 'He's a big lad. Let's see if he can do a man's work before we judge him.'

Dunham's dark eyes glowered. He muttered, 'We'll see what weight the toddler carries . . .'

Chapter 28

They had just arrived at the beginning of the Old Road. Mr Sampson's phone rang. He took the call, and then moved away from Josh to talk privately. Josh scanned the area around. All the men were climbing up the hills, to get into position.

He had a moment to himself. He knelt, and took Reggae's head gently in his hands. He looked into her soft, eager eyes. 'It's pretty amazing we're here at all. Just show them what you can do.' She licked his face, her tail wagging furiously.

Josh unhooked the lead from her collar. Reggae looked off to their right. The first group of sheep was coming down the hill.

'This is it,' Josh thought.

'Away!' Reggae raced off to his left to get behind the sheep, just as he'd trained her.

* * *

The men on the hills were taking a lunch break. They'd all brought sandwiches and thermos flasks with tea. In the rush to get out, Josh had completely forgotten about food, though he'd remembered water and biscuits for Reggae. It was no different from a normal school 'lunch', he consoled himself.

But he soon realised that while it was easy enough for the men on the hills to take a break, it was different for him and Mr Sampson. There were already more than a hundred sheep on the Old Road. It was their job to keep them there, and not let them disperse. This was even more difficult now that they'd stopped moving the sheep forward while the other men had lunch.

When Josh had stopped for a moment to fill up Reggae's water dish, ten sheep had made a dash for freedom, heading back up the hill. He'd had to send Reggae racing to bring them back. He could see that Mr Sampson's hands, and Bobby's feet, were similarly full.

Eventually, Josh managed to get some water, and a couple of treats, into Reggae. But she was definitely beginning to flag. She was used to a long nap in the middle of the day while he was at school. No chance of that today.

In a rare quiet moment, he wondered why the vet had put them on the road. It must be the most testing of all the positions. Maybe that was it. He was giving Josh a chance to prove himself to the crofters. He looked at Reggae, who was still gamely bringing sheep down the hill and keeping them together on the road. He hoped it wasn't too much for her.

* * *

The day had passed quickly, in a blur of sending Reggae off to get sheep, and working with her and Mr

Sampson on keeping the sheep on the road. Now they were nearing the pens where the sheep would be held. Several dogs from the hill had joined Reggae to keep the large group of sheep together. Josh and Reggae had stayed at the back, to prevent stragglers. This was no easy task, as every few feet a ewe would find a patch of grass very interesting, or a group of lambs would head off up the hill to play with one another.

So far, the day had gone well. They'd managed to avoid any contact with Dunham and his dogs. Now, he was coming down from his position halfway up the hill. He passed close to Josh.

'Your pet,' he spoke quietly, so that only Josh could hear, 'looks like she's on her last legs. She'll die of a heart attack before the day's over'.

Reggae growled at Dunham, but he just strolled over to the front of the flock, where he started rolling a cigarette and speaking to a friend.

Josh watched as Reggae raced around, trying to keep the sheep moving forward. She *had* looked really tired earlier in the afternoon. Could Dunham be right?

Then he reminded himself that Borders had been bred to run all day. And Reggae's tail was wagging constantly. Surely she wouldn't be having a whale of a time if she were near death . . . He relaxed.

The area they were passing through was one they knew well, as it was on the way to the second valley where they'd trained. Patches of bramble alternated with sharp outcrops of rock.

Reggae barked once. She was staring up the hill, at the area Dunham had left. At first, Josh thought that Reggae was just excited at recognising a place she knew. But then he saw a slight movement in a patch of bramble. Dunham's dogs had missed one of the sheep.

Josh shouted to attract Dunham's attention. But he was too far away, and too involved in his conversation, to hear. Josh didn't want to leave a single sheep behind. And besides, this was a chance for Reggae to shine.

'Do you think you can get her? You'll have to move fast because we don't want to lose any of these.'

Reggae's eyes were eager. 'Away then.' Reggae streaked up the hill.

The older man who was working near Josh, watched smiling as Reggae headed off. 'She's seen a rabbit, I bet. The young ones can't contain themselves all day.' He called his dog to take Reggae's place at the back of the sheep. His Border was eight, old for this kind of work. 'She's done well. A real natural dog.'

Josh was sure he'd seen this man before – where was it? That's right! He was in the charity shop talking to the owner when he was buying Reggae's bed and bowl. He'd bought Reggae her first bone!

'I don't think it's a rabbit.'

Then several things happened at once. Reggae flushed the sheep out of the bramble patch, and started moving her down the hill. The man talking to Dunham looked back and saw this. He said something to Dunham, who turned and then threw his cigarette to the ground, furious. He shouted at his dogs, who streaked off after Reggae and the ewe.

Then everything went into slow motion: One of Dunham's dogs got between Reggae and the sheep. Reggae growled to warn him off. Dunham's dog attempted to nip Reggae, but she dodged past him. The ewe, suddenly surrounded by three dogs, froze with fear. Everyone, it seemed was watching the drama on the hill.

'That'll do,' Josh shouted. Reggae immediately retreated from the ewe, to give it space. But Dunham's dogs, caught up in the excitement and their master's anger, ran towards the ewe. One jumped up on her back, just like it had done to his uncle's sheep in the secret valley. Terrified, the ewe started back up the hill. Then she disappeared from view.

It seemed everyone was shouting at once. Had Josh blown it? Just as he was on the verge of success? He didn't have time to think. All the noise had disturbed the sheep on the road. Smaller groups started moving away. Josh called Reggae back, to help keep them together. She obeyed instantly. Reggae and the old man's dog settled the sheep, while two other crofters and their dogs brought in the ewe that Reggae had found. Fortunately, she wasn't injured.

But the arguments about what had happened on the hill continued until the sheep arrived at the pens. Josh kept silent, not wanting to make the situation worse. In any case, he suspected no one would listen to a twelve-year-old boy.

*   *   *

After all the sheep had been penned for the night, the vet called a meeting. Yvonne was standing with her dad, looking worried. Josh was pretty sure he hadn't done anything wrong. But Dunham was well known and much feared. Who would speak up for him?

'We all want to get home for dinner,' Neill said. 'But we need to sort out what happened on the Old Road.'

Dunham snarled, 'The boy was out of order. His stupid little pet was working my patch. If that ewe had been hurt it would have been down to him.' He addressed the vet. 'You shouldn't have let a boy work the Gathering. He shouldn't be back tomorrow.'

Several of Dunham's mates muttered agreement. Josh sensed that others disagreed, but were afraid to speak against Dunham. But if no one spoke soon, the vet might think it had been Josh's fault!

After a brief silence, it was Mr Sampson who spoke up. 'Mr Redlin is just plain wrong. Before he sent his dog off, Josh tried to get his attention – but he was too busy smoking and talking to his friend to notice.'

Josh was grateful Mr Sampson had said something. But he could see that his words didn't carry much weight – he was just a teacher after all, not a crofter. Josh needed someone with more authority to speak for him. Otherwise, everything would be lost.

Dunham looked around at the assembled crofters with an intimidating look. Then he smiled. Everything was going his way. He was going to get his revenge on Josh.

Then the old man who had worked near Josh at

the end entered the circle. 'I was watching the boy and his dog all day,' he said in his soft voice. 'The young dog did a great job with the sheep. I was right there when she spotted the stray.'

Everyone seemed to be listening intently to the old man, as if he were some kind of VIP on the island. Josh was puzzled. If he was so important, how come Josh didn't know about him?

'As Mr Sampson said, the boy called to Dunham. But he wasn't paying attention. It was only then the boy sent his dog off. He was right to do that. If he'd left the ewe out there, and it was infected with the parasite we're going to treat, she could have reinfected the whole herd.

The old man turned to face Dunham.

'People miss sheep on the hill all the time. That young dog had control of it. It's no pet. You were wrong to make it personal. You almost hurt a good dog and a good ewe.'

Josh could see Dunham didn't like being addressed like this. But he liked what the old man said next even less.

'But maybe you can help me. That ewe your dogs brought in. It had an unusual wound on it, two bite marks near the bottom of the spinal cord.'

That's a strange way to speak about a ewe's rump, Josh thought, as he listened intently.

'The boy's dog never got near the ewe. But your dog . . .' he didn't finish the sentence. Then he went on, 'I've noticed quite a few of the sheep we've brought in have similar wounds.'

194

A crofter Josh knew only vaguely spoke up. 'Some of *my* sheep escaped onto the commons for a couple of days. Two of them had a wound like that.'

Everyone's eyes turned on Dunham. Josh's 'offence' had been totally forgotten.

Dunham looked hard at the crofter who'd just spoken, and then at the old man. 'What kind of crazy rumour are you trying to start? There's all kind of wild animals on the commons that could have done that . . . Nobody has ever seen my dogs hurt any sheep.'

As Josh watched Dunham, he saw his eyes widen slightly. Yes, Josh thought. Be afraid. Somebody *has* seen your dogs hurt some sheep. Me.

Dunham gave Josh a menacing look. Josh smiled.

Dunham's fate was in *his* hands. For a moment, he enjoyed the sense of power. But it reminded him of what he'd felt when he'd shamed Kearney. And he'd promised himself he would never do anything like that again.

Besides, if he spoke now, everyone would want Dunham's dogs put down. It wasn't *their* fault they hadn't been properly trained. And surely, after this, Dunham would have to make sure they never hurt another animal.

So Josh said nothing. The group fell quiet as people took in what had happened. He imagined they were making a mental note to inspect their own sheep for wounds on the rump.

The vet turned to Dunham. 'The two people who had the best view disagree with you about Josh and his dog. The matter's closed.'

195

He turned to the other crofters. 'It's been a good day. Go home and have dinner. And a well-earned dram.'

The crofters chuckled appreciatively.

'I'll see you all here at Romesdal at 8 o'clock tomorrow morning.'

The men headed back to their cars and jeeps, talking animatedly in small groups. Josh knelt down and rubbed Reggae's tummy. Hamish, who'd witnessed the argument between Dunham and Josh at the beginning of the day, paused by them. 'The two of you did well. Carried a man's weight. See you tomorrow.'

'Thank you,' Josh said, suddenly full of feeling. He had hoped the men would be fair. And they had been. Except for Dunham and a couple of his gang. 'Up, girl,' he said and Reggae stood. She was shaking with fatigue. Josh suddenly realised he too was exhausted. Adrenalin had kept him going all day, but now it had run out. They had a five-mile walk in front of them.

'You two look done in,' Neill said. 'Would you like a ride?'

Josh looked at him gratefully. 'I hadn't realised how much it would take out of her.'

'And yourself, I suspect,' Yvonne's father replied. 'I'm glad you had a chance to meet Dr James.'

Josh was puzzled. 'Dr James?' he asked.

'The man who spoke up for you,' Neill explained. 'He was the island vet before I came.'

That's why everyone had paid attention!

'My van's over there.'

Yvonne was standing by it. Reggae recognised her and raced over, her tail wagging. Josh followed.

He stuck out his hand, awkwardly. Yvonne looked skyward and rolled her eyes. Then she gave Josh a warm hug.

'You did it!'

'So far, so good,' Josh said. He was aware the third day of the Gathering, up on the cliffs, was the most dangerous. And he still had Day Two to get through before that . . .

'Let's get home and fed,' Neill hurried them along.

That sounded great to Josh. But *his* day wasn't finished. He had a difficult conversation ahead of him. One which would decide Reggae's future.

Chapter 29

The sun was still shining as Josh tied an exhausted Reggae to the fence outside his uncle's house. There was no point in trying to keep her secret any more. Either Calum had already heard about her, or he would in a minute.

Josh paused outside the front door. He looked fondly at Reggae, then beyond her to the loch at the bottom of the hill. The tide was in. He examined the water. He knew he was just delaying the moment of reckoning. But maybe he'd see a dolphin – that would be good luck.

But even his sharp eyes couldn't pick out a dolphin in the flat water. He sighed and turned towards the door. He couldn't put it off any longer.

'Wish me luck.'

He entered the house, stopping for a moment to remove his boots in the hallway. Then he went on to the kitchen.

Calum was bustling around, preparing dinner. Josh could see he'd made an effort. There were several pots on the cooker, and he could smell roast chicken in the oven. His favourite.

'We have to talk,' his uncle said, without taking his eyes off the roast potatoes he'd just removed from the Aga.

So he knew.

'Do you mind if I have a wash first?'

Calum looked at him for the first time. Josh tried to read his face – he didn't *seem* angry . . .

'Of course not.'

Calum always washed off the day's dirt and sweat before eating. But it wasn't just that. Josh needed a moment by himself. All the tension and emotions that he'd kept in check had suddenly hit him. He and Reggae had accomplished so much. Surely, it couldn't all go wrong now . . .

In the bathroom, Josh took off his T-shirt and cleaned himself with a flannel. He climbed up to the loft and found a fresh shirt. Then he returned to the kitchen.

Calum was serving out the food onto their plates. Josh suddenly realised he was starving. He knew Reggae must be hungry too, but this wasn't the moment to ask to feed her. Not while her fate was still undecided.

As usual, they sat in silence. After their years of living together, Josh could usually read his uncle's moods. He still couldn't *see* any signs of anger. Rather, he would swear his uncle was upset. Really upset.

Josh stared at his plate. Up until this moment, he hadn't really considered Calum, or how he'd feel when he discovered Josh had kept a dog secret from him. The only thing that had mattered to him was keeping Reggae.

For the first time, he imagined what it must have

been like for Calum . . . to hear from *someone else* about how Josh had joined the Gathering with a sheepdog he knew nothing about. His uncle was a terrible liar, but to save face he would have pretended he'd known. But what must he have *felt*? Humiliated? Shamed? Betrayed?

His mind went back to the conversation with the vet. 'Are you sure you want to do it this way?' That must have been what he was trying to tell him. That he was just thinking about himself.

In spite of the appetising smells that filled the kitchen, and the plate of roast chicken in front of him, Josh suddenly wasn't hungry.

He remembered his first meal here in this kitchen. It had been roast chicken too. And just like now, his uncle had been silent. It wasn't at all what Josh was used to. Reggae music blaring out of his mother's cassette player, her chatting away or inventing games to encourage him to eat his vegetables . . .

He was, he recalled, *scared* of this big, silent, serious man. He hadn't understood why his uncle wasn't talking to him. And he'd decided it must be because his uncle hated him. Hated being saddled with a skinny, sad, seven-year-old city boy.

Had he ever stopped being scared?

He was frightened when he brought his school reports home – though all his uncle ever did was to try to find something positive to say. He was anxious when he had to ask for new shoes, or a bigger jacket for his school uniform, even though his uncle never refused. And of course, hadn't he hidden Reggae's existence from Calum for so long because he was scared of what he'd do?

Josh glanced furtively at the other side of the table. Calum's plate was almost as full as his own. He must be pushing food from side to side too . . .

Josh felt a sick feeling in his guts. He couldn't remember his uncle *ever* losing his appetite.

He'd made this gentle man an enemy, and for what? For being used to eating alone? For not being able to buy him everything he wanted? Or for not being as warm and funny as his mother?

'Someone who does a man's work needs to eat like a man,' Calum said softly.

Even after all this, his uncle's voice was gentle. He looked, *really looked*, at his uncle. His head was bowed, as if he'd been crushed by a heavy weight.

He'd done this – by not trusting Calum to be fair. Without thinking, Josh jumped up from his seat, and ran over to the other side of the table. And for the very first time, he hugged Calum. He blinked back tears.

'I'm so sorry,' he said. 'I didn't mean to hurt you. I just wasn't thinking . . . of you. Just about keeping my dog, Reggae.'

'There, there,' Calum said, patting Josh on the back awkwardly. 'You did what you thought best.' His voice was thick with emotion.

After a bit, Josh sat down and stared at his food, his heart still heavy.

'My sister . . . she loved reggae music, didn't she? You named your dog after that . . .' Calum said.

'"Reggae",' Calum said the name hesitantly, as if trying it out in his mouth, 'must be hungry.'

'I'm sure she is.'

He climbed up to his room and found Reggae's bowl and the secret cache of dog food. When he came down, his uncle was standing.

'Let's see her, then.'

They went out together. Reggae was fast asleep. But as they got nearer, the smell of food woke her. Her tail started to wag. Josh filled the plate and put it down in front of her. Reggae waited. 'Go,' Josh said. He saw his uncle smile slightly. Then his uncle knelt down and tickled Reggae under the ear as she ate.

'Small, isn't she?'

'I think she was the runt of the litter. I found her by one of the rivers on the commons.'

They watched Reggae finish the tin of food.

'You rescued her,' Calum said, getting the picture. 'And you knew how I felt about pets.' There was a deep sadness to his voice. As if he felt misunderstood. And hurt.

'I should have asked,' Josh said. 'I should have asked properly.'

His uncle blinked as he ran his finger down the bony bit between Reggae's eyes. She closed them, enjoying the attention. After a bit, Calum nodded slightly, almost to himself. 'I hear "Reggae",' he said the name a bit less hesitantly, 'did really well today.'

The words just rushed out of Josh. 'She did everything I asked. Even things we'd hardly had a chance

202

to practice, like gathering a singleton. We were on the Old Road and she drove the sheep and kept them together like nobody's business.'

'She must have had a good trainer.'

'It wasn't me,' Josh protested. 'She's just a natural dog.'

'Even natural dogs need good trainers,' Calum persisted. 'How did you learn?'

'There's lots of videos on YouTube. And lots of advice on the web and in forums. And the library had two books too.'

From Calum's puzzled look, Josh realised that he didn't know what forums were. Or YouTube for that matter. Josh took some time to explain them, and to answer his uncle's questions. He didn't want to exclude Calum from anything to do with Reggae, ever again.

'You've been very resourceful and very ingenious.'

Josh blushed.

'. . . The patience I learned from you helped too,' he said.

Calum looked at him, surprise written all over his face. It was as though it had never occurred to him that Josh might learn anything from him.

'I've tried to be a good . . .' his voice trailed off.

'You *have* been!' Josh protested. 'I just never . . .'

Then neither of them said anything for a while.

Calum broke the silence. 'You didn't bring the sheep in using Polo mints . . . Or save the scraps for a wounded animal . . .'

'I *hated* lying to you. It's just that I had this plan

– I had to keep her secret until she proved herself at the Gathering.'

He was just making excuses. He owed Calum more than that. 'I was a coward. I'd understand if you wanted to punish me.'

Calum looked at Josh a long time. 'It was wrong to lie to me. But now you're taking responsibility for what you've done.' He paused. 'At your age, that's all I can ask.'

Josh leant over and hugged his uncle again. 'I promise I'll never ever do anything like this again.'

Josh felt Calum tense. Maybe he didn't like being hugged. Josh let go. 'I'm sorry.'

'It's not you, Josh. It's just that my family . . . we weren't very physical with one another.'

Josh gazed at Reggae and thought about his mum. How she had hugged him and kissed him at every opportunity. She must have been trying to be different with him from how she was raised . . .

'We have some decisions to make,' Calum continued. 'Like where we put the kennel.'

Josh could hardly believe his ears. 'Do you mean it?'

Chapter 30

The last day of the Gathering was the one crofters dreaded. It started on the cliffs and was the severest test of man and dog. An over-eager dog could cause sheep to panic and go over the edge. And dogs had been lost when the crumbly cliff face dissolved under their feet as they tried to get behind a lamb at the cliff's edge. Josh had had nightmares about it.

But it was an opportunity for Reggae to prove herself, and for him to complete the Gathering and make money to help Calum with her keep.

He'd never spent any time on the cliffs with Reggae because getting to that part of the commons involved them crossing a major road, and then a forest which walkers and tourists used a lot. The cliffs and the rocky land leading up to them were just beyond the forest.

Josh and Reggae had been promoted to the top of the cliff. Dr James, the old vet, walked with him as they climbed to their starting point. Josh had discovered his first name was Hugh, but he didn't feel it was right to call him that.

'It's a compliment to you and your young 'un,' Dr James was saying. 'But unless I miss my guess, she isn't used to cliffs.'

'We've never been up here.'

'The cliffs are a wild and beautiful place. But they're dangerous too. Especially for those who don't know their ways. Let my experienced dog lead the way today.'

'Thank you,' Josh said, relieved.

For some reason, Josh didn't feel shy with Dr James. He plied him with questions about what a vet would do in different situations.

But every so often Josh had to interrupt him because Reggae was drifting too close to the cliff's edge. She was totally without fear, and just didn't seem able to let another dog – even Hugh's old Border – gather 'her' sheep.

'Come Reggae. Now!' Josh shouted for the tenth time that day. When Reggae returned, reluctantly, Josh scolded her. 'If you don't listen, I'll have to put you on the lead.' He removed the lead from his rucksack to show it to her. She brushed against his leg and rolled over on her tummy.

'Don't try to get around me,' Josh warned affectionately. 'Just two more cliffs and then we'll head down to the pens. Stay with me.'

Then Josh spotted a ewe and two lambs just up ahead, grazing on a patch of grass near a rocky outcrop.

Josh headed up the hill, keeping his hand on Reggae's collar. He could get behind the sheep himself, and walk them down a safe distance. Then his dog could take over. But as Josh was approaching the small group, a rambler dressed in a bright red jacket appeared on the other side of the outcrop. The

lambs panicked, and skittered to within feet of the cliff edge. The ewe bleated, and headed after them.

'Steady!' Dr James shouted from along the cliff. 'Give them a moment to get used to everyone.' Josh stopped. So did the rambler, who seemed to realise the delicacy of the situation. Josh kept a tight grip on Reggae's collar. After a few minutes, the ewe and lambs had relaxed enough to start grazing.

It was then that Josh saw the sea eagle, dropping out of a cloud above and to their right. It was a large one. And it was swooping towards the sheep. In his mind's eye, Josh saw what the eagle intended – to pick up a lamb, lift it over the cliff edge, and then drop it, where it could feast on it at leisure. Josh's brain went into turbo overdrive. If he shouted or let Reggae go, the little group would panic. They *all* might go over the edge.

Josh couldn't see a solution that would be safe for the sheep – and for Reggae. So he just held on to her. He could only watch as the eagle swooped down, lifted a lamb by the neck, then dropped it onto the rocks below. Startled, the ewe and the other lamb raced down the hill.

Josh let Reggae go after them. Dr James joined him and they walked up to the cliff edge together. The lamb was still. Josh felt awful.

Dr James put his hand gently on Josh's back. 'You saw it coming, didn't you?'

'Yes,' Josh said, ashamed. 'I was afraid to let her go.'

'You did exactly the right thing. If you'd released her, we would have lost all three, and maybe the young pup too. The eagles are part of the natural order too. We can spare a lamb or two for those magnificent birds.'

'I've always thought of them as my enemy,' Josh said, surprised. 'They want to eat the little animals I rescue.'

'They have as much right to dinner as we do.'

They started down the hill together. 'You've an old head for such a young lad. You're always watching and learning.'

'That's because I have a lot *to* learn! But I do like watching, especially animals. All of them have their different ways.'

'That they do,' Dr James agreed.

*　*　*

They drove the sheep they'd gathered into the pens.

'Good work, Josh.'

'See you tomorrow, Josh.'

'Tomorrow the hard graft starts, right Josh?'

The first day, the crofters had all referred to him as Calum's boy. Now they called him by his name. That felt good. And yet strangely, after the other night, he felt more like Calum's boy than ever before.

Josh bent down to give Reggae a rub. Dunham appeared. He hadn't approached Josh since the first day of the Gathering. The vet had kept them working in different areas.

'You were right to keep quiet to protect me,' he rasped.

209

Josh stood so that he could look Dunham straight in the eye. He felt a confidence he'd never known before. 'I wasn't protecting *you*,' he replied. 'Just your dogs. It's not their fault their owner didn't train them properly.'

Dunham stared at Josh, as if he couldn't believe his ears. Then his face flushed.

'I've trained more dogs than you've had winters.'

Josh raised his eyebrows. 'I hope your other dogs weren't as vicious as the ones I've seen.'

Dunham's face turned an even darker red. But Josh had had enough of the sour man's anger. He called Reggae and started to walk away.

'Don't you . . .' Dunham snarled. Josh glanced back. Dunham had stopped mid-sentence because he'd clocked that a group of crofters were looking at him. A moment of fear crossed the man's flushed face. Josh guessed he was wondering if they'd over-heard the conversation.

He turned away, pleased he'd won this small victory. He knew this wasn't the end of the matter. He had an enemy for life. Still, he wasn't going to let this bully spoil his sense of accomplishment. The Gathering couldn't have gone better. He and Reggae had set out to prove their worth. They'd accomplished that, and more.

He had leftover chicken to look forward to. And there was a lot to tell his uncle after dinner.

Chapter 31

Josh pulled out the last remaining blanket from the shed.

'You want to keep this smelly old thing?' he asked Reggae.

She grabbed it with her teeth and pulled on it.

'I'll take that for a yes, then,' Josh said, his voice smiling. He gazed at the old broken-down shed. 'We've had some good times here, haven't we, pup?'

But Reggae was too excited to sit and talk. She started towards the house, dragging the blanket with her. She wanted it in her new kennel.

* * *

Josh and Yvonne sat in the afternoon sun, with Reggae between them. Josh was rubbing Reggae's tummy and Yvonne stroking her cheek. Reggae was almost purring.

Behind them was the new kennel he and Calum had built in the croft's front garden. It had space for Reggae to lie in the sun while Josh and Calum were away, and a rear compartment which was sheltered from the wind, rain and snow. She loved it.

Suddenly, Reggae leaped to her feet and started barking. She took her new role as watchdog very seriously. And she liked being able to bark now that she wasn't a secret dog.

Josh looked up and was surprised to see the vet at the gate.

'Oh!' Yvonne exclaimed. 'He must have finished early!'

Josh didn't have time to react, as Yvonne's father approached, holding out his hand. Josh got up and shook it. 'Hello, Mr . . . Neill,' he said awkwardly.

Neill smiled and admired the kennel. 'I do prefer the home-made ones . . . Is your uncle home?'

Josh nodded.

'I'd love a cup of tea.'

*   *   *

The four of them sat around the kitchen table with their mugs. As ever, the kitchen was dark. But unusually, Reggae had been allowed to come in with them. She sat at Josh's feet, occasionally licking his ankles.

The vet took a sip of his tea, and nodded to Calum. He leant over and took a white envelope from his briefcase. He handed it to Josh. 'We've just settled the fank accounts.'

Josh tore open the envelope and found a cheque for £600. He was stunned.

'The prices for the sheep were good this year, and the crofters voted you a full share. It was almost unanimous.' Josh could guess who had voted against him. 'But I had to write the cheque to your uncle because, legally, you're not old enough to work.'

Josh had dreamt of this moment, of having his own money, of the things he could buy. But, much to his surprise, he found himself saying, 'I owe Calum much more than that.'

Calum looked down at the table and blinked rapidly. Then, after a pause, he said, in a gruff, thick voice. 'Don't be daft, boy. We'll open a bank account for you. You've earned it.'

Neill continued. 'The men were full of your praises. They said you were strong and not afraid of hard work. And that you were a natural stockman.'

Josh blushed. He knew that was the crofter's highest compliment. 'It's not me,' he blurted. 'Reggae's just a natural dog.'

'And that got me to thinking,' the vet continued, as if Josh hadn't said anything. 'I'm not able to get around like I used to. I've got arthritis in my knees and hips.'

Josh *had* noticed that the vet moved with difficulty, wincing often.

'Yvonne tells me saving animals is your passion. And Hugh told me how impressed he was with you and that you were interested in what it was like being a vet.'

Why were Yvonne and Calum smiling at him? Did they know something he didn't? Some secret?

'What I'm getting at, in my long-winded way, is that there's a lot of heavy physical work involved in being a vet. I just can't do it any more. I need someone to help me.'

Josh still didn't get what Neill was driving at.

Neill looked Josh in the eye. 'I was wondering if you'd be willing to help on some of my rounds. Maybe after school a few days a week and some time at the weekends. Of course, we'd have to work out a way for you to get paid until you're officially old enough to have a job, and you'd also have the chance to learn more about helping animals.'

'Me?' Josh asked, his mouth open. 'You want *me* to help *you*?' He looked at Yvonne. 'Yvonne already does that. And I'm sure she's better at it than I would be.'

Neill smiled. 'Of course, Yvonne's invaluable. But she's five foot nothing, and the cows I need to manhandle into place weigh over 1000 pounds.'

'I couldn't,' Josh said. 'I've got to help Calum on the farm. And besides, I'm not smart enough.'

'We could do it together,' Yvonne urged.

Josh's head was reeling.

Calum said, 'It's a great opportunity, son.'

'Are you sure?' Josh asked his uncle. 'You can't do everything around the croft yourself . . .'

'I'm not planning to,' Calum said. 'You'll still have to do your homework, *and* help around the croft.'

Josh looked around the table. He gradually realised that Calum had known that the vet was going to ask him to help. And so had Yvonne. All of them had known! Except him.

Everyone was smiling at him encouragingly. Like they were a family. The one he'd never had.

He stood up, unable to contain himself. 'Did you

hear that Reggae?' Reggae rose to her feet, her tail wagging.

'I'll take that as a "yes",' Yvonne's father said, in a deadpan voice.

'Definitely. Yes! Yes! Yes! Thank you, sir!' He looked at Yvonne. And without thinking gave her a quick hug. She blushed.

Not wanting to be left out of all the excitement, Reggae leapt up and licked Josh's face. Josh held her against him, as Reggae licked his face again.

'This is all down to you,' Josh told her. 'My super, secret dog!'

Acknowledgements

Some years ago, my family visited the Isle of Skye for the first time. We stayed with Yvonne White and Joe Curran, who run a small croft and B&B outside Portree. Their place became the inspiration for Uncle Calum's croft. And the idea for *The Secret Dog* came out of a late night conversation between Joe and the now retired Skye vet, Neal Stephenson.

I have a golden retriever who will occasionally sit when I command, but no one would say I was a great dog trainer. To make the dog training in the book accurate, I needed help from real dog trainers, and I was lucky to find Julie Hill and Nij Vyas. Julie showed me how a master works with a well-trained dog, and Nij gave me my first experience of working with border collies. Julie also read all the bits of the book about dog training to correct any mistakes I made.

Neal Stephenson was the inspiration for the vet in the book (though he wouldn't recognise himself or his van!), and he answered some of my many questions. But I felt I needed to see a vet in action. Dr Iain Muir generously agreed that I could spend a day with him. I watched him doing operations and saw what happened when he did rounds.

My writer's group – Candy Gourlay, Helen Peters

217

and Christina Vinali – read many early drafts of *The Secret Dog* and their suggestions improved it enormously. Cliff McNish, who joined the group after I'd finished the book, read it as a whole and offered many helpful suggestions.

Others who read the book at various points and who offered valuable comments include Sarah and Hannah Beskine, my daughter, Susie, and my wife, Julie. I owe a special thanks to Susie, without whom I would never have written a single children's book, and to Julie, who is my rock in days when writing and life are not going well.

I don't really believe you can send a children's book out into the world without reading it aloud to a real child first. Ana Rock was a great audience, and I could tell from the moments when her attention wandered which bits needed rewriting.

Finally, my wonderful agent, Lindsey Fraser, not only found my publisher, Birlinn, but also made valuable suggestions that improved a later draft.

Joe Friedman
March 2015